Praise for
The Broadway Ballplayers

"Inspirational stories . . ."

—*Los Angeles Times*

"The Nancy Drew of sports . . ."

—*Chicago Sun-Times*

"Sports aren't a pastime—they rule . . . Holohan uses sports to help her characters learn about life. . . . This is not Barbie . . . it's much closer to what you can see in your driveway or local park."

—*Chicago Tribune*

"The stories . . . delve into other issues, including friendship, relationships with parents, gender stereotypes, and social status."

—*Kansas City Star*

"A great series for girls and boys in sports or who want to be in sports!"

—PMA/Benjamin Franklin Awards

"It is encouraging to see stories featuring girls who play sports . . . and play sports well. . . . Give this series a try."

—*VOYA*

"Truly exemplifies what sports and life are all about. . . ."

—Dani Tyler, 1996 Olympic Gold Medalist

Books about the Broadway Ballplayers
by Maureen Holohan

Friday Nights by Molly
Everybody's Favorite by Penny
Left Out by Rosie
Sideline Blues by Wil
Don't Stop by Angel
Ice Cold by Molly
Catch Shorty by Rosie

CATCH SHORTY
by Rosie

Series by MAUREEN HOLOHAN

Aladdin Paperbacks
New York   London   Toronto   Sydney   Singapore

To those who, regardless of height,
always stand tall.

First Aladdin Paperbacks editon August 2002

Text copyright © 2002 by Maureen Holohan

ALADDIN PAPERBACKS
An imprint of Simon and Schuster
Children's Publishing Division
1230 Avenue of the Americas
New York, NY 10020

The text of this book was set in Concorde BE.
Printed in the United States of America

10   9   8   7   6   5   4   3   2   1

Library of Congress Control Number 2002101672
ISBN 0-7434-0748-2

Chapter One

My mother always told me that it's not the size of the lion in the fight, but the size of the heart in the lion. At five feet two inches, she marched down the sideline, cupped her hands around her mouth, and never let me forget the lion. "Heart, Rosa!" she yelled. "Heart!"

While one parent took things in stride, the other grew frustrated by me being closer to the ground than other kids. My father kept telling coaches and parents that I was just about to hit a huge growth spurt and traced it back to his grandmother's sister, who grew almost six inches in one summer back in 1911. When he bugged me about eating right and drinking my milk, I went into my room and put on my headphones. I cranked up the volume hoping the music would wash away the feelings of not being tall or good enough. But the songs always ended, and the feelings came back.

I didn't say much about anything until my father came home from work one day and told us that he had taken a new job and we were moving. With the first girls' football league about to kick off, the Ballplayers and I had a chance to make history. My team needed me and I needed them.

My family could go on without me. Broadway Ave. was my home, and that's all there was to it.

I watched the clock and waited for one last tick. Sitting at my desk at school, I gripped my books and set my feet on the ground. *Tick, tick . . . BEEP!* I jumped up and darted toward the door. Miss Lopez looked up from her textbook and snapped it shut. She glared at me as I zipped across the room. I half-smiled. "Please read tonight!" she said firmly. "And that means you, Rosalinda!"

Yeah, yeah. Whatever. I liked Miss Lopez because she was young and played sports. I loved her English class for the simple reason that it was the last class of the day. The only annoying thing about Miss Lopez was that she had this thing about kids reading something besides school work for thirty minutes a night. I asked her one day if reading a cereal box counted. She said no. I asked about the comics. She shook her head.

"Rosie, did you hear me?" I heard her call out as I reached the hallway.

I knew I couldn't get away with a nod of the head, so I ducked my head back in the classroom and said softly but loud enough for her to hear: "Yes, Miss Lopez."

I hit the checkered hallway of Lincoln School and felt free as a bird. While other kids stopped to socialize, I dumped my books into my locker and waited for my best friend, Scotty "Sleepy" Jackson. I glanced right and then left. I stopped and watched two girls toss a shoe back and forth over Billy Flanigan's head. He kept jumping and missing the shoe.

"Give it back!" Billy yelled.

The girls stared down at Billy as he trembled in anger.

"Come on," one girl snickered. "Can't you get your shoe back?"

I crouched down by my books until she cocked her arm. When she let go, I sprung up and reached out for the shoe. I grabbed it with one hand and then wrapped it up with the other. I clenched it tight in my hand as the girls stood with their mouths wide open.

"Come on, Rosie," one said. "You're no fun."

I glared at her, handed the shoe to the tearful Billy, and returned to my locker. Billy caught his breath and mumbled, "Thank you." I turned around and tried to smile, but there was nothing to be happy about when you were picked on for being short or slow or different. I pulled my hat out of my locker and flipped it on backward over my head. Then I looked up and spotted my best friend, strutting down the hallway with his loose arms swaying at his sides. Nobody had eyes as droopy and cheeks as chubby as "Sleepy".

"I just talked to Penny and Molly," he said. "They said Beef and Cowboy and J. J. want to play at the park. They want to know if you're in."

I nodded. "You're playing, right?"

He puffed out his cheeks and shook his head.

"Why not?" I asked.

"I think it's boys against girls," he said. "I hate it when they play like that."

"What?" I gasped. "We mix up the teams most of the time."

"I don't know," he mumbled.

My mouth dropped open. This wasn't the play-all-day-and-night kid I knew. We'd spend nights in the pouring rain throwing the baseball around and running through a swamp from one base to another.

"What's wrong, Sleep?" I asked.

Just as I said it, Pete the Creep walked by us and I cringed. He leaned close to Sleepy with his beady eyes and smelly breath. Then he whispered something in my best friend's ear. Pete held his hand up trying to cover his big mouth. He tipped his head back and snorted in laughter.

"Get outta here, Pete," Sleepy mumbled in frustration. "Nobody asked you anything."

Pete left and I turned to Sleepy. "Are you gonna tell me what's wrong?"

He looked past me and his eyes grew wide. "Mr. G.'s coming!"

I swiped my brother's baseball cap off my head and stuffed it into my bag. "Miss Jones!" Mr. Gordon's voice bellowed. My muscles tightened. "I'd like to have a few words with you."

I hung my head, knowing the way Mr. G. asked for those few words meant trouble. Sleepy slipped on his coat and grabbed his books.

"Wait for me," I said.

"I can't," he replied.

"Come get me before you go to the park."

My best friend didn't look at me.

"Rosie Jones," Mr. Gordon called out. "May I have a minute?"

I walked over to our school principal and looked straight up.

"Did I see you with a baseball cap on your head?" Mr. Gordon asked.

The truth was the only way to stand a chance with Mr. G. "Yes," I said quietly.

He stuck out his hand. "May I have it, please?"

I shook my head nervously. "I'm sorry," I said. "I promise I won't do it again."

I felt so incredibly small standing next to the most powerful man in the building. It didn't help that our principal stood about six and a half feet and lifted weights like a pro football player. "Hand it over," he said. "You know the rules. I'll keep it until you prove you understand the rules."

"I'll bring you three from home, but please not this one," I begged. "It's from the big leagues. Rico gave it to me."

He huffed and gave me a rare glimpse of his soft side. "Do you promise not to break the rules again?" he asked.

I nodded even though I didn't feel that wearing a hat indoors was as criminal as Mr. Gordon made it out to be. I just smiled and thanked him for letting me off the hook. He asked how my brother Rico was doing with his professional baseball career, and I replied with an "okay." That's pretty much all I knew. Then he asked another question that required a more complete answer. "How's English class?" he said.

"Umm," I said. "Good."

He pressed his lips together and raised his eyebrows. "What does good mean?"

"Everything is fine," I said. It was the truth. I wasn't failing or getting into any trouble.

"I'll be sure to ask Miss Lopez if there is anything that will help make English class great for you," he said.

I just wanted to leave the building, go home, and burn off all of my sixth-grade frustrations down at the park. Instead I was stuck in an interrogation and being threatened with a background check.

"Have a good afternoon," Mr. G. said, and then he moved on to the next student.

I racewalked down the hallway and tried to catch up with Sleepy. Just as I spotted him, my redheaded friend Molly O'Malley called out my name.

"What's up, Ro?" Penny Harris asked as I walked over to my friends.

Wil Thomas gave me a low five, and I smiled at the Ballplayers from our home street—Broadway Ave. Penny "Sweet P." Harris, who was the coolest kid in the city, gave me a big, cool smile. The only person missing from our neighborhood group was Angel Russomano, who had moved on to the high school.

"Are you playing today?" Wil asked.

I nodded. "Of course."

"Let's get going before all the eighth graders get there," Molly said.

"What's wrong with eighth graders?" Wil asked defensively.

"They think they run the show around here," Molly explained.

"Whatever," Wil said dramatically.

"And they have such attitudes," Molly added.

"Don't even get me started," Wil said firmly. "You are Miss Attitude."

Penny ignored all the cracks. Molly, Wil, and most of the kids on our street went back and forth between slinging a range of gentle sarcasm and harsh insults. Everybody did this except Penny and me. Penny just smiled and shrugged most things off. Not many kids insulted Sweet P., because she was not only cool and fun, but also a phenomenal athlete. Although hardly anyone picked fights or arguments with me, most kids called me Shorty and cute one too many times. Unlike Molly, I usually didn't retaliate with any bad words or muscle. But there were a few exceptions.

"The boys want to play against the girls," Molly announced.

"Why are they into this girl-boy thing all of a sudden?" Penny asked.

"They know we mix up the teams all the time," Wil pointed out.

"They say girls can't play football," Molly said, rolling her eyes. "You know I handled that well. Pete made me so mad I wanted to stuff the football in his big mouth."

"I don't even want to get into some battle of the sexes," Penny said.

"I hear that," Wil agreed. "What's the point? Why do

we even have to prove anything? They already know we can play."

"Kick their butts is more like it," Molly added.

"Yeah," Wil said. "Don't they know how Jackie Joyner-Kersee, Billie Jean King, and Babe Didrikson put an end to all these stereotypes? I'm telling Mr. G. that we need to enhance our history classes with some women-in-sports material."

Molly looked at Wil, and voiced my exact sentiments. "I'm all for this women's rights stuff, but can we leave the lesson plans in school and just play?"

"That's the only plan I'm thinking of right now," Penny said. "Let's take care of this at the park."

Chapter Two

I raced home and called Sleepy on the telephone.

"What's wrong?" I asked.

"Nothing," he insisted.

"Are you ready to go to the park?"

"I'll meet you down there," he said.

We always walked down to the park together, so I knew something was up.

"Well . . . I guess I'll see you there," I said, hanging up the phone.

I wished my brother was home. He and Sleepy hung out all the time. Maybe Sleepy would tell Rico what was going on. I poured a glass of iced tea and snacked on a handful of pretzels, hoping the phone would ring and it would be Sleepy saying he was sorry. My mother was due home any minute, and I had to get out of the house before she started quizzing me about my homework. I cupped the pretzels in my shirt, bent over, and stepped into my cleats. Pulling up my hood, I took one last look at the phone and then scooted out the door.

As I jogged down Broadway Avenue in the fresh fall air, I watched the kids come from all directions. The flow of traffic on the sidewalks led to the corner of Broadway and Woodside, which was the home of our very own Anderson Park. I sprinted the entire way, ignoring the sounds around me. My focus was up in the distance, on my friends and the fun waiting for me. I pushed the thoughts of Sleepy, Miss Lopez, and Mr. G. out of my mind. It would soon be game time with the older kids. I had to be ready to play.

Pete turned around after catching a pass. Then he stopped and watched me jog onto the field. As I grew closer, I could sense him getting ready to strike. "Hey, Shorty," he said to me. "You think you can handle playing with the big boys today?"

I scowled at the creep and wondered who invited him to play at our park. He didn't live on Broadway. He had no right. I turned to Jeffrey "J. J." Jasper. I liked him because he never called me small or short. He couldn't. He was the smallest eighth grader in the class. I watched J. J. joke around with Eddie Thomas, who had claimed the infamous title as neighborhood bully. I wanted to walk up to them and ask why Pete the Creep was polluting our air.

"Let's go!" Penny said.

"Yeah," Wil added. "I've got people to see, places to go, and things to do!"

"We already made teams," Pete said. "Boys against girls."

Molly's freckled face flushed red. Wil pushed her glasses up and then rested her hand on her hip. Penny coolly adjusted her headband, turned to Pete, and asked, "How many hours have you spent playing at Anderson Park, Pete?"

"So?" Pete shot back.

"We're the veterans," Molly said as she moved closer to Pete. She stared him in the eye and moved even closer. She pointed to herself with her thumb and said, "We make the rules."

I grabbed Molly's arm and pulled her away. She tried to shake my hand off, but I held on.

"Shut up, Molly," Pete said and he pushed her aside.

Molly scoffed and looked around in disbelief. "I'm going to pretend that you didn't just push me," Molly said as she waved her palm in his face.

"How can you just come on down here and think you can call all the shots?" Wil yelled, and then she shook her head. "You've got nerve, man. And I don't like it."

"Football is a sport for men," Pete said.

Penny looked right and left. "I don't see any men here, do you, Ro?"

I just stood there looking up and around at everybody, afraid of what was going to happen next.

"You missed me, P.," J. J. said with a goofy grin as he threw his shoulders back and chest out. J. J. usually played park comedian, but this time nobody laughed. I looked around at Pete, Eddie, Billy, J. J., and Mike. I stared, wondering how many of them really thought that football or any sport was only for boys and men.

Then I saw Beef Potato, Cowboy, and Sleepy walking over the basketball courts and in our direction. "Who needs some real football players?" Cowboy called out.

We all cringed at his timing and his wrong choice of words. Cowboy's head bobbed right and left, and he dipped his shoulders as he strutted along. We called him Cowboy because he dressed up as one for Halloween and the name stuck. His partner in crime, Beef Potato, was nicknamed by his older brother for his stocky frame. I looked at Sleepy and he quickly glanced up at me and muttered, "Hi."

"Boys against girls!" Pete repeated.

"Fine with me," Cowboy added.

An all-out ten-person shouting match followed. It came to the point where nobody could hear anyone else. One struggle led to another. Molly was mad at J. J. for not standing up for us. Eddie told her to relax. Wil didn't think Eddie had the right to butt in and that it was between Molly and J. J. Eddie told Wil she was doing the exact same thing. Cowboy started laughing at all of us, which made things even worse. Pete the Creep had started the fire, and it was spreading out of control.

"What is wrong with you?" Molly screamed at J. J. Her voice cracked. "I thought you were our friend."

"You're the one who—"

"I never expected you to be like this," Molly said, cutting him off.

J. J.'s jaw dropped open, shocked that Molly would insult him so easily. Penny stuck her fingers in her mouth and whistled so loudly that I had to cover my ears. As if she had waved a wand, in a split second everyone froze.

"We're all playing together," she said calmly. She took another deep breath, which meant she was really mad. "Two-hand touch, so nobody—boy or girl—gets hurt. Football is meant to be played in pads. If you don't like it, then go home."

I turned to Pete. He rolled his eyes and looked around for some kind of support, but nobody gave him any respect. Despite his attitude he stayed put, which meant he had agreed to play by our rules. Penny split up the teams, and we started our game.

When Penny didn't put me on her team, I wanted to go home. Then I looked over at Pete standing beside me, and I could think of nothing worse. Pete begged to play quarterback, but Cowboy overruled him.

"You're not a regular down here, man," Cowboy said. "Do your time first, and then maybe you can be 'the man.'"

Then Cowboy looked at me. "Or 'the woman,' I don't want to start that war again."

We played for an hour or so without any more arguments. Cowboy passed to Molly and handed off to me as much as anybody else. It had nothing to do with making sure we all had a fair chance. Cowboy could throw, Molly could catch, and I could run. We needed all of our players to win. But we didn't. Sweet P. led her team with perfect passes, and Beef Potato and Wil cleared out holes as wide as streets for J. J. to run through. On one play J. J. tried to fake me left, but I read it, stayed low, and smacked him with all ten fingers and two hard palms on his back.

"Agh!" he yelled as he fell forward. "When did you get so strong, Ro?"

I grinned. But on the next play he scored, and Penny's team won 21–7. I hated to lose as much as the next Ballplayer, except Molly, who would probably make herself run laps or do push-ups as a personal form of punishment.

As most of the kids left the field, the Ballplayers and I hung out while Molly cooled off. Angel slowly walked over to us. Her feet, sore from soccer and running, had put her on the sidelines for a few weeks. We asked how she was doing in high school.

"Fine," she replied.

"You're lying," Wil said to Angel. "You miss us and really should have stayed back a year."

Angel laughed. It felt good to see her smile after hearing of all the treatment and pain she'd been through with her feet. "What'd you play today?" Angel asked.

"Football," Penny replied.

"You should have heard the boys earlier," Molly said. "Pete the Creep started saying how football is only for men."

"It's over," Penny said. "We proved our point."

"How many more times do we have to prove ourselves on our own turf?" Wil asked. "I'm with Molly on this one. We've got to do something."

"Forget the boys," I said.

Everyone turned to me in surprise. No, I didn't speak much, but I couldn't stand to see this dispute continue for another second.

"If the boys are playing in their own leagues," I began, "then why don't we make our own?"

"Against the boys?" Wil asked.

"No," I said. "Let's just form our own girls' league."

"Yeah," Penny said with a smile. "We could send some flyers around school and get enough players around here and maybe on the East Side for a league."

Molly wiped the dirt off her face with the back of her sleeve. "It sounds good to me."

"Separate but equal?" Wil said. "I don't know. We don't have any equipment, no footballs or coaches. We don't even have any rules or regulations."

"Can't you figure that part out?" I asked her.

She looked at me with an eager grin. "Are you challenging me, Ro?"

I shrugged, not knowing what I was doing.

"It's a challenge for all of us," Angel said.

"Has this ever been done before?" Molly asked. "Full pads and everything?"

We all turned to Wil. She looked up, wincing at the sky as if she were flipping through the pages of history. "Not that I can recall."

"We could make history!" Molly said. "Wouldn't that be cool?"

We all agreed until Penny shared a word of caution. "Once the boys find out, they're going to be talking that boy-girl nonsense again."

"J. J., Mike, and Billy won't say anything bad," Molly said.

"Neither will Sleepy, Beef, and Cowboy," I added.

"But kids like Pete will start talking like they're

football buffs," Penny pointed out.

"Pete thinks a nickle and dime are what they flip before the game starts if they don't have a quarter," Wil says. "He just runs his mouth because he thinks he has the right."

"Uh, Wil," Molly says. "What *are* the nickle and dime?"

"Defenses, Mo! Don't you watch *Inside the NFL*? Where is your head?"

Before Molly could retaliate, Angel jumped in and kept us focused. "I think we should go for it," she said.

"Yeah," Molly said. "Forget Pete and all the other idiots out there. We're playing."

We all turned to Sweet P. She grinned. "Let's do it."

Later Sleepy and I walked home. I wanted to tell him about our football league and how excited I was that I was the one who came up with the idea. But I waited for him to offer some information on why he was acting so strange.

A bike zoomed past us. Pete looked over his shoulder and called out, "Walking your girlfriend home, Sleepy?"

Then Pete snickered and sped away. I wanted a crack in the sidewalk to reach up and trip him. Sleepy walked silently, and I waited until I couldn't take it anymore.

"That's what's been buggin' you, right?" I asked.

He didn't respond.

"Kids are making fun of you for hanging out with me, aren't they?"

"I tried to tell them that we're just friends and that we grew up together," he said. "But they don't get it."

I didn't say anything. If Sleepy truly felt he couldn't handle the pressure, then I didn't want to be his friend anymore.

"I'm sorry for acting so stupid," he said.

I waited for an explanation, a solution or something. Anything that would make me feel like this struggle would not come back to haunt us.

Chapter Three

I flipped through a baseball magazine later that night. Every few minutes I glanced up at the television and then went back to my magazine. I wished Miss Lopez could have seen me. She probably would have said something about the TV being on, but at least I was reading. One day I told her how many books I had read over the summer on Roberto Clemente, who was my favorite baseball player of all time. She said I should look for books on female baseball and softball players, too. I searched the shelves for three days, but couldn't find any.

"I'm going to have to say something," she had said.

I looked up at her, silenced by her passion and frustration.

"Isn't it unfair that there aren't any stories in this library about girls and women like us?" she asked.

I nodded. Then I actually thought about what she had said. She was right. It wasn't fair. "What can we do?"

"I'll get the librarian to order some right away."

"Good," I said.

"And maybe someday someone will write a book about you," my teacher told me. "Or you can write your own life story."

I thought about Miss Lopez and smiled. At school her straight black hair was pulled back in a plain barrette. She usually wore dress pants and sweaters and a few nice skirts. But after school she traded her barrette and school clothes for a hair elastic and a sweatsuit. Some afternoons I spotted her leaving through the side door to start her daily jog. She always told us how much she loved sports, especially baseball and football.

"I played against my brothers all the time," she'd told me.

She wore hardly any makeup, which made her even more beautiful. All the kids at school always wanted to ask if she had a boyfriend or was looking to get married soon. She never answered. I guess it was none of our business. But I kept thinking about the chances of Miss Lopez and my brother Rico going out together. *They could coach our football team! Yes! It will be perfect!*

Then I stopped and thought about potential problems. Rico skipped college and went straight to the pros, which was something Miss Lopez would not see as acceptable. *But so what? He is still a good guy. Maybe she can convince him to go back to school. Then they'd get married and I could brag to all the kids at school that Miss Lopez was my sister-in-law.*

The door creaked open and I looked up at my brother. Rico smiled as he slipped off his shoes and dropped his gym bag. He had been working out to stay in shape for another shot at the major leagues. He took off his hat and slicked back his sweaty black hair.

"Hey, kid," he said to me.

I smiled. Although I didn't have any books about other girls in sports, I had a brother who never treated me any less than anyone else. I loved it when he took me to the batting cages with him and showed me hard work. A few times I tried to match him push-up for push-up, sit-up for sit-up. One day I did fifty-eight push-ups in a row in front of all of his friends.

"You staying for dinner, Ric?" I asked. The smell of my mother's sweet and spicy chicken hung heavy in the air.

"I'm going out to dinner with Natalie," he replied as he headed down the hall. I sank back down into the sofa thinking about Natalie and her bright red bows and heavy eye shadow. My mother called her a sweet girl, but I wanted to know what else she could do besides stand next to my brother and show off her teeth.

"You're not giving her a chance," my mother always told me.

With great women like Miss Lopez out there, I didn't understand why my brother had to see Natalie all the time. But during the baseball season, Natalie always took a backseat. Then again, on some days, I was right back there with her while baseball drove Rico's life.

I eagerly waited for my brother to finish showering and return to the living room so I could tell him all about my football league idea. I finished reading one article and then picked up the sports section of the paper. I dropped it down from in front of me when I heard my brother's quick footsteps.

"Gotta go," he said. "I'm already a half hour late."

I watched him, hoping that he would change his mind and stay home and eat with his family and not some wimpy girl. He opened the door and slipped on his coat. The cool fall breeze carried the scent of his cologne across the room.

"Hey, Dad," he said as he looked up.

My brother left and my father walked inside, which was a common occurance in our house.

"Guess he has more important places to go," my father mumbled. The tone of his voice and the dark lines under his eyes kept me quiet. He said hello to both of us as he loosened his tie.

"Just in time," my mother called out. "The chicken is ready."

I pushed myself up from my seat on the sofa and walked behind my dad. He stood six feet tall and claimed to have been quite an athlete back in high school. I could tell by the way he tossed a baseball that he knew how to play. But his shaky jumpshot on the basketball court told a different story. One day I came close to defeating him in a shooting game for the first time ever.

"Still can't beat your old man," he had said.

"I came pretty close," I replied.

"Close only counts in horseshoes and hand grenades," he said.

My face had felt hot. He never said "good game" or "nice shot." With every year that passed, he came down harder on me to excel in sports. His occasional outbursts at games and outspoken comments about coaches and players hurt me more than words could say.

The hardest thing was that he wasn't always so stern and demanding. He taught me how to play checkers and poker. He also took me to car shows and told me how much money you could make if you took care of something over a long period of time. I loved it when he taught me things about business, insurance, and money. But when he snapped about my missing a grounder or a jumpshot, I caught a glimpse of a person obsessed with perfection and winning. He turned into a man I didn't want to know.

My mother was her own sort of perfectionist. Although she didn't work full-time, she juggled a few part-time jobs and hobbies at once. She zipped from her job as a secretary to the salon, where she and her sisters and cousins spoke Spanish and laughed at jokes as they cut hair and gave manicures. Then she'd come home and stay up until all the dishes were out of the sink and the laundry was under control. A painting of San Juan, the small statue of the coqui frog, and plaques of Puerto Rican proverbs decorated each of our five tidy, dust-free rooms.

As I entered the kitchen, I proudly told my mom and dad about my pitch for the first girls' football league. My mother looked up from her plate and raised her eyebrows.

"Football, Rosa?" she asked.

"We're going to have a tackle league just for girls," I said.

"Tackle?" my dad repeated. "I've never heard of that for girls."

"We're not doing that powder puff, two hand-touch thing," I said. "That's for wimps."

"Football?" my mother repeated.

I nodded and said, "Yep. The game for the insane. That's what Wil calls it when it gets really dangerous."

My mother looked like she was about to throw up. "I dreaded every day your brother went to football practice," she said. "I don't think I can handle this."

I turned to my dad. I needed him with me on this one.

"You've got pads, right?" he asked.

I nodded.

"Do you need a coach?" he asked. "I played football back in my day. Strong safety, punter, wide receiver, and back-up quarterback."

I didn't answer right away. I weighed the risk of having him coach my friends. I could imagine him telling Wil to use "her big body" or for Molly "to stop being such a baby." He'd say something like that and hurt kids without even knowing it.

"I think we're going to coach ourselves," I said. "Or Miss Lopez is going to help out." I needed some wishful thinking to help buy me some time.

After dinner I updated my parents on how well I was doing in school. I told them I had been reading a little more because Miss Lopez would be all over my case if I didn't.

"I like that Miss Lopez," my mother said.

The Broadway Ballplayers

After dinner I went to my room. When I finished my math homework, I grabbed my mitt and started tossing the ball up into the air. I reached out and flipped up a bad toss and then dived on the ground, trying to catch it. I got down in my ready position. Legs shoulder-width apart, glove down, and all eyes on the imaginary batter. *Crack!* I flipped the ball up, snagged the line drive, hit the floor, and acrobatically rolled back up on my feet.

"You'd better be finished with your homework," my mother called out.

"I am!" I yelled back.

My mom and dad started to argue over what Rico was up to and how he didn't do enough around the house. I'd heard it all before, so I put my headphones on. As I started looking through my baseball cards, I thought of Sleepy. Ten minutes later I decided that I just needed to talk to him. He was my best friend, and I didn't like not getting along. I pulled my headphones off and walked out of my room. I froze when I heard a few words from the conversation my parents were having in the living room.

"I don't want to move," my mother said. My heart skipped a beat. I tiptoed down the rest of the hallway and pressed my back against the wall. I leaned close to the corner and listened.

"The pay will be better," my father said. "We'll be able to afford a bigger house."

"What about the kids?" my mother asked.

"Rico's got his own thing going," my dad said. "Rosie's a good kid. She'll make the adjustment."

What? Are you crazy? No, I won't make any adjustments! How could he even think I'd want to leave our street and our house? I wanted to run right out in the middle of the room and tell them to stop this nightmare before it got any worse. But my mind kept telling me not to believe it. My ears had heard wrong. They wouldn't do this to me.

I returned to my room and lay flat on the floor and continued my game of catch. Later I awoke when I heard my bedroom door open. I looked up and saw my brother.

"What are you doing on the floor?" he asked.

I tossed my glove and ball off to the side and slowly pushed myself up off the ground. I picked up my hat and flipped it backward on my head, just like him. Then I collapsed on my pillow. Rico said good night and began to pull the door shut.

"Wait!" I called out. "Don't go!"

He pushed the door back open and looked at me.

"Did Dad say anything to you about moving?" I asked.

"What?" he asked.

"Dad's taking a new job and selling our house," I explained.

He shook his head. "I haven't heard anything about it," he said. "I don't think Mom and Dad would leave this place."

"But that's what he said."

"Don't sweat it, kid," he said as he sat down on my bed. "You've got school and your friends to worry about."

I thought about Sleepy and decided now was not the time to get into our personal struggles.

"We're starting a football league," I told Rico. "Will you coach us?"

"How's the pay?" he asked with a grin.

"Please," I begged. "Mom will feel better if you're there. And if you coach, Dad won't have to."

He sighed and said he'd think about it, but that he might need some help. It wasn't a good time to mention Miss Lopez. Not yet. But when I thought of her, I remembered the magazine I had been reading on the couch earlier and wanted to show him something. I took off and passed the kitchen table on my way into the living room. I froze when I saw a brochure of houses for sale. I picked it up. Anger rushed through me as I raced back to my room.

"Look!" I said to my brother. I threw the brochure on my bed. "They can't be serious, can they, Rico?"

Chapter Four

I overslept the next morning. When I saw the time on the clock, I ran out of my room to see my mother before she went to work. I needed some answers to the moving rumors. She was on her way out the door when I walked into the kitchen. She hurried across the room and bent down so her face was even with mine. "I'm running late," she said, and then she kissed me on the forehead.

"I wanted to talk to you," I muttered.

"We'll talk later."

I stared at the floor.

"Hurry, Rosa!" she said as she walked away. "Don't miss the bus!"

I stood at the table and took a few mouthfuls of cereal and one big bite of toast. When I heard my father's heavy footsteps, I sat straight up in my chair.

"Good morning," he said as he passed by the table. Then he looked at his watch. "You're going to be late for the bus, aren't you?"

I stared at him as he picked up the paper and opened it to the sports section. I wanted to ask what was going on, but nothing came out. My muscles went tight. Fear rushed through me. I jumped up and raced to my room. *This isn't happening! This isn't happening!*

Three minutes later I was out the door, jogging down Broadway Avenue. Each identical small house seemed to have a life of its own. I looked down the alley and caught a glimpse of the O'Malleys' beat-up old basketball hoop nailed to a telephone pole. The kids from Broadway spent hours under a dim spotlight, shooting hoops and rolling bowling balls into the garbage cans.

I looked up and spotted Mr. Miller, an old man who had lived on Broadway Avenue his entire life. He tipped his hat and smiled as he took his daily stroll. I halfsmiled as I stared past him to the Uptown Apartments. The Ballplayers and I didn't spend a lot of time inside the Uptowns, mostly because Wil always hustled us outside. Wil's high-rise had earned a bad reputation for having run-down living quarters and broken families. I don't know why she was so embarrassed. I wouldn't exactly call my family perfect. Even Angel's parents had problems, and her dad was a minister.

Out of all the kids on Broadway Ave., Penny seemed to have the most going for her: a great family, good grades, athletic skills, and a future. A lot of kids hung around with Sweet P., maybe hoping that some of her skills and good luck would rub off. Penny quickly picked up on the way kids befriended her after wins. She could also tell when they wanted her to hang out with them just so they could be part of the cool crowd. Penny never complained too much about others. She just stuck with her friends. Win or lose, success or failure, the Ballplayers stayed together, which is exactly why I wasn't going anywhere.

When I spotted the dirty yellow school bus, I hit full stride. I stared straight at the door, knowing all eyes inside the bus were on me. My lungs felt like they were going to explode as I skipped up the steps. I turned the corner, adjusted my cap, and spotted Sleepy. I plopped down in the seat next to him.

He pointed to his watch and said, "You set the record for the fastest sprint from the telephone pole to the bus stop. I'm going to have to beat it tommorrow."

I panted and grabbed the cramp in my side. But I was happy to see the old Sleepy. Penny looked up over the seat in front of us.

"Hey, Ro," she said. "Did you ask Rico to coach us in football?"

"He didn't give me an answer," I said. "But he'll do it. What do you think about asking Miss Lopez, too?"

"Yeah," Molly said. "She's cool."

Wil peeked around the seat behind me and started talking strategy. "How are we going to make teams?" she asked. "We need a fair way to let everybody play."

"How about a draft?" Penny said.

"That might be complicated," Wil said thoughtfully.

"Wil will find a way," Molly added with a grin.

We all stopped and considered the options for a

moment. Wil took an extra few seconds and then blurted out, "I got it!" We all turned and looked at her.

"We'll make up a flyer and post it at school," Wil said. "All girls interested in playing in the first girls-only football league report to Anderson Park on Friday."

"But we don't have any coaches, uniforms, or equipment," Molly said. "We have nothing."

"Except dozens of girls who want to play," Penny pointed out. "That's all that counts."

"Depending on how many girls show," Wil continued, "we'll nominate a set amount of captains who will hold a draft. We'll run through some drills so we can check out who's got skills."

"Sounds good to me," I said.

"But you know how ugly things get when people pick teams," Penny said. "It becomes personal."

"If you can't take it, then you don't deserve to be in the league," Molly declared.

"Yeah," Wil added. "This is all business."

Molly made a list of all the contacts we could think of who might be able to get equipment, and Wil was in charge of draft-day scheduling and events. Penny said she'd leave Angel responsible for making up the rules. Then she turned to me. "What do you want to do?"

"Yeah," Molly said. "Speak up, Rosie."

I sat there letting this conversation fly past me. All I kept thinking was how much I loved hanging out with my friends. We did so many fun things together. Nothing or nobody could take me away from this. I didn't care if my dad was asked to be president. I wasn't moving anywhere.

"What's left?" I asked.

"How 'bout you convince Rico to help coach?" Penny said. "And ask him if he has any friends who want to referee the games."

"Most of Rico's friends won't work for free," I explained.

"We'll tell them that the check is in the mail," Wil joked. "A little volunteer work won't hurt anybody."

"I'll ask Miss Lopez if she'll help us out, too," I added.

"Wait a second," Molly said. "If we have a draft, we might not all be on the same team."

Wil rolled her eyes. "We'll trade players, and provide some other incentives to get who we want. Agents and teams in the big leagues do it all the time."

"You're forgetting something," Molly said. "They play with real money."

Wil and Molly argued back and forth. Some of the boys stuck their nose in our conversation and laughed. I looked at Sleepy to make sure he didn't dare snicker. He just stared out the window. I elbowed him in the side.

"What?" he asked.

"What's bugging you now?" I asked. I couldn't understand why my friend was becoming so difficult.

"Nothin'," he said.

"What do you think about our football league?" I asked with excitement.

"It's cool," he said softly.

Then Pete the Creep yelled from the back of the bus. "Sleepy and Rosie sitting in tree . . ." He whined the song like a baby.

Molly stood up and screamed at Pete, "You're pathetic!"

"Sit down, Fat Stuff!" he yelled back.

Penny stood up and glared back at him with the don't-even-start-with-me look. When Sweet P. stopped smiling, rotten kids like Pete stopped and went the other way. I stared straight ahead. My muscles grew tighter and my face felt hot. I hoped that Sleepy didn't feel the embarrassment. Out of the corner of my eye, I watched Penny sink back down in her seat. Not another word came from the back of the bus. I peeked at Sleepy out of the corner of my eye. His sad eyes stared out the window.

By the last class of the day, the buzz about the girls' football league was the talk of the school. I skipped into Miss Lopez's room early to ask her to be part of a once-in-a-lifetime opportunity. She looked up at me as I came in, and her eyebrows furrowed. "I needed to talk to you," she said.

The tone of her voice knocked the wind out of me.

"Your classwork hasn't been where it should be," she began, "and a lot of your assignments have been late."

I reached in my folder and whipped out my home-work.

"The work you hand in looks like you finished it on the bus," she added.

My chest felt tight and my palms began to sweat.

"You haven't put your best effort into anything this year, and I'm going to make it my job to personally see that you do."

I stared down at the ground ready to explode. She didn't know that I had my father looking over my shoulder all the time. She didn't know how mad I became at my mother for letting him treat me this way. She didn't know that my family might be moving.

"Was there anything you wanted to tell me?" she asked. "I kind of cut you off before you had a chance to say anything."

I mustered some strength and for the sake of the league, asked her to be part of history. "We're starting the first girls' football league."

"You are?" she said with an excited smile.

I nodded. "Will you help?"

My teacher grinned cautiously. "Help?" she asked. "How?"

"We could use another coach."

"How many teams are there in the league?"

"We don't know yet," I replied.

"When do we have practice?" she asked.

I shrugged. "We haven't talked about that yet," I muttered.

"Any other coaches?"

"My brother," I said. "He's really cool."

She stared handing out papers to kids as they rushed inside the room. "I don't know, Rosie," she said. "Sounds like I'm getting myself into more than just a coaching job. I don't know if I have time to run the whole show."

"You don't have to," I said. Then I pointed my thumb to my chest proudly. "We're doing most of the work."

Miss Lopez pushed her hair behind her ear and focused her attention to the stack of papers on the desk. Then she looked up and took a count of all the kids in the room.

"Please take your seats," she called out.

I moped back to my desk. For the entire forty minutes my thoughts wavered between moving out of the city and whether I really truly wanted Miss Lopez to be a part of our football league. She'd be on my case all the time about homework and reading. As cool as I thought she was, I didn't know if I could handle her nagging me at practice, too. When the bell rang, I tried to slip out, but Miss Lopez called my name. I listened with my back to her.

"Turn around!" she said.

I slowly faced my teacher. "If you rewrite these homework assignments by tomorrow," she said, "I'll think about coaching."

I smiled and nodded.

"From here on out, you must put more energy and time into each assignment. No more doing your homework while watching the TV or with the radio on."

I looked up wondering how she knew my study habits.

"Concentrate on English," she ordered. "Or you're going to have more problems than not having a football coach."

I nodded because it was the right thing to do. As I left the classroom, I flipped through all the homework I had to rewrite for English class, which would take me all night. I started thinking that maybe I had gotten the raw end of the deal. I kept my head down as I stressed about all my work. I turned the corner and ran right into two eighth graders. Our collision sent my papers flying. I mumbled an apology and then started picking up the sheets.

"Watch where you're going, Shorty," one said.

"We almost didn't see you," the other added.

I stood up and glared at them both.

"Hey," one girl said as she got a closer look at me. "You're a Ballplayer, right?"

I nodded.

"Then you must be trying out for that football league," she said.

I didn't say anything.

"What a joke," she said. "I know that I'll make it if a shorty like you is trying out."

The two girls looked at each other and laughed. All at once, the stress of school, football, and moving came down on me at once.

"I dare you to show up Friday," I said. "You won't be able to touch me. Count on it."

They looked at each other and rolled their eyes like I was some sort of freak or weirdo and kept walking. As other kids stared at me, I began to feel stupid for talking a big game.

"What's wrong, Ro?" somebody asked me.

I looked up and saw Penny. I wanted to dump all my worries about Miss Lopez, the stress of moving, and how much I hated people calling me short. But I didn't want her to think I was a baby.

"You're not beginning to act like Molly, are you?" Penny joked.

I exhaled and flashed a half-smile. As I walked off

with the coolest kid at Lincoln School, I felt as if a huge weight had been lifted off my back.

"They started it," I said.

"Then you finish it," Penny said. "On the field."

I couldn't wait for my chance.

Chapter Five

I waited patiently for almost twenty-four hours, pretending that I didn't know anything about the secret being kept from me. Yet every time I looked at my mother, I waited for her to tell me to pack my bags because the moving truck was on its way. If they dropped the bomb on me, I'd fall to the ground kicking and screaming. No, I'd run away. Yeah. I'd just grab my ball and mitt and take off down the street. Rico would be the only one who stood a chance at catching me. But I knew the alleys and hiding spots on Broadway Ave. so well that neither he nor anyone else would ever be able to track me down unless they called in the canine unit. I'd hide out until they left and went on with their lives without their only daughter and sister. Then I'd move into Sleepy's basement. He would sneak me food and bring me baseball magazines. Nobody would ever know I was there.

Just before my father came home, the phone rang. I jumped to it, hoping it was Molly giving me the inside scoop about the football draft, but it wasn't. It was a man with a friendly voice.

"Hello," I said hopefully.

"Hello," he responded. "Is this Rosie?"

"Yeah," I replied.

"How are you today?" he asked.

"Fine," I mumbled to the stranger.

"Is your father home?"

"No," I said. His friendly attitude made me suspicious.

"Could you please tell him that Frank called from the real estate agency?" he said.

My heart sank. My nerves tingled. I lost my breath.

"Can you do that for me?" he asked.

"Yeah," I muttered just before I slammed the phone down.

When my father walked through the door, I refused to look at him.

"Who was on the phone, Rosa?" my mother asked, entering the room.

"Wrong number," I replied.

As my dad set his briefcase on the floor, my eyes wandered over to him. I knew his briefcase was filled with real estate books with pictures of houses that could never be mine. Tears came to my eyes as I thought about some other kid taking over my room and staring at the fluorescent stars that my brother had stuck on the ceiling. Nobody could just come into our house and strip it of all its personality. Every pillow, stuffed animal, and portrait had a place and history of its own. I stared around at everything and couldn't hold it in any longer.

"Are we moving?" I asked.

My mother fumbled the plastic cup in her hand. My father froze as he loosened his tie. He turned to me with his eyebrows raised. "Where would you get that idea?" he asked.

I glared back at him. I didn't get all A's in school, but I was not stupid. "I saw the pictures of all the houses," I said firmly. "I heard you and mom talking."

My mother and father stopped and stared at each other.

"You didn't even ask me!" I blurted out.

"It's not up to you," my father replied.

"This is my life, too!" I yelled. I jumped up, wanting to head toward the front door, but my father stood too close. I stormed out of the room and down the hallway.

"Wait!" my mother said. "Come here, Rosa. We need to talk this through."

I kept walking. My mother sprinted toward me, grabbed my arm, and pulled me back into the room. I tried to resist, but she kept pulling. When I realized how mad she was, I let up. I stumbled over to the table, a bit surprised that my mother had so much power.

"Sit down!" she ordered. Then she stared at my father. "You, too!" He pulled up a chair and we all sat down at the table. My mother took two deep breaths and began. "I don't want any more secrets."

"What secrets?" my father asked. "It's none of her business!"

I was out the door and down the street so fast that I didn't realize I was without a jacket or sweatshirt until I ran past Molly's house. My mother knew I had a habit of fleeing stressful situations. So the second I was out the door, she grabbed the keys, jumped into the car, and beat me to my spot. I stopped in front of Molly's house and stared at the ground. My mother pushed open the car door.

"I'm not going back," I said.

She sat and waited.

"He's not making us move!" I yelled. "It's not fair!"

"I feel the same way," she said quietly.

"Then why aren't you telling him?" I asked.

"I'm trying to keep an open mind for what is best for our family," she said. "Please come in the car so we can talk about this."

A chill swept under the back of my thin T-shirt. I took two steps and slipped inside our car.

My father was chewing a mouthful of mashed potatoes when we walked in the door. He swallowed and wiped his mouth. I clenched my fists and walked past him and headed toward my room.

"Please have a seat," my father said calmly.

"I don't want to," I said.

"Rosalinda Jones!" my father's voice boomed. "Have a seat!"

As if he had thrown a lasso around my body, I turned around and headed toward the table. I crossed my arms and did not face him. He took a deep breath and then began. "We are looking at houses in another city because I might have a chance at a big promotion. We'd

40

be able to get a bigger house and have a big yard. Maybe we could even get a dog."

"I don't want a dog," I said.

My father sighed. "Look, Rosa, nothing is set in stone. I don't know about the job and won't know for a while. We're looking just in case."

"I don't want to go," I said.

"We're a family," my father said. "So we're in this together."

From that point on, I threw talking out the window. I had to think of some other strategy to end this nightmare. And I needed some help.

I reported to Anderson Park Friday afternoon at four P.M. sharp. I jogged through the maze of seventh- and eighth-grade giants, ducking underneath elbows and dodging receivers as they warmed up. I looked to the right and spotted one of Molly's biggest rivals—Tasha from the Hawks basketball team. She threw the ball like a missile. It stuck to her receiver's hands. The receiver turned toward me with full cheeks and a tiny grin. I smiled. It was Sheila, our friend from the basketball league. She squeezed the ball with both hands so hard that I thought it was going to pop. Her thick arms bulged and her grin grew wide.

"Hey, Jonzie," she squeaked. "What's up?"

I shrugged and asked, "Where are Molly and Penny?"

"Over there," she said as she pointed. Then she looked at me again with one eyebrow raised. "Are you trying out for this league, too?"

"Yeah," I snapped defensively. "Why?"

"I was just asking," Sheila said. She threw the ball back to Tasha.

I eyed my friend suspiciously, wondering if she laughed at my size behind my back. But I stopped short of thinking bad thoughts. Sheila was cool. She wasn't like the big-mouths and troublemakers who had nothing better to do than make fun of others. I jogged away from Sheila not saying goodbye, but didn't worry about being rude. If Sheila hung out with Tasha, who was a full-time motormouth and all-star show-off, she obviously didn't take attitude problems personally. I ran in the direction of the Ballplayers, eager to see my friends.

Penny, Molly, and Wil stood in a tight huddle. Streaks of mud ran along Molly's blue sweatpants and sneakers. I couldn't imagine how she managed to get dirty before practice started, but that was Molly. Wil, who was always cold, had a hat pulled tight over her head. Penny had on matching red sweatpants and hooded sweatshirt. On any other kid, the outfit would have looked ordinary. With her magnetic smile and hip-hop style, Sweet P. always stood out in the crowd.

"Hey, girl," she said to me as I ran right into their huddle.

"What's up?" I asked.

"You ready to play?" Molly asked. A smile snuck out of her as she looked right and left, nervous that one of the other players would see her acting less than serious. "This is huge!" Molly whispered loudly, strugging to hide her excitement. "Everybody is here!"

"We're going to be famous!" Wil shrieked and then she giggled.

"Play it cool," Penny said. "We've got a lot of things to do."

"But P.," Molly insisted. "We are big time!"

"Who has ever heard of a girls' football league started by girls themselves?" Wil asked. "We're go-getters, leaders, women of the new millennium. Feel the power!" Wil looked up to the sky and threw her hands up in the air. She squeezed her eyes shut under her blue-rimmed glasses and screamed. Penny and I burst into laughter.

"Excuse me, Miss Power," Penny said with a smile. "But we've got over fifty girls here who are starting to ask questions. Do you have a plan?"

Wil rolled her eyes and rested her hand on her hip. "Do *I* have a plan?" she scoffed. "Of course I have a plan." She reached into a gym bag and started filling out a chart. "I've got almost everybody signed up already. I have everyone's name on a slip of paper in this box so we can pick captains." We watched as she pulled out a tissue box.

"Then what?" Molly asked.

"We're going to do drills so the captains can see who can play," Wil explained. "Just like in the pros. We need some scouting time."

We all agreed to Will's plan, so she reached into her bag and picked out a whistle. She blew on it and everybody stopped. "Bring it in, ladies!" she yelled. "Let's get this show on the road."

"Do you really think this is going to work?" I whispered to Penny.

She shrugged. "I hope so."

"I don't know how many girls are going to listen to somebody our age," I said.

"Me neither," Penny agreed.

One by one, girls started to walk our way. Nobody smiled or sprinted with enthusiasm.

"Hustle!" Wil screamed.

"Yeah," Molly muttered.

The group kept walking. Wil shook her head and hollered, "We don't look ready to play, ladies!"

"All right, Commissioner," Penny said. "We hear you."

I looked at Penny and shrugged again. After a few more seconds all the girls at the park huddled around the Ballplayers. Wil cleared her throat and raised her voice above the crowd. "First I want to thank everyone for showing up," she said. "I was worried that some of us would forget."

"You called us all three times," one girl muttered.

"And you put posters in every stall in every bathroom in our school," another added.

"I just wanted to make sure everyone had a fair shot," Wil said.

"Is everyone here playing?" Tasha yelled out as she smacked her gum.

"Yes, I'm going to explain every–" Wil began.

"That's stupid," Tasha said, cutting her off. "There should be tryouts."

Wil adjusted her glasses nervously. Molly glared at Tasha.

"We're going to have four captains," Wil announced.

"Do captains get to pick their teams?" a girl asked.

Wil nodded.

44

"I want to be captain!" Tasha said.

So did just about everyone in the crowd. They all started whispering back and forth and then yelling their comments at Wil. She responded as quickly as she could, but the complaints kept coming. I turned to Penny, who put her fingers in her mouth and let out one of her paralyzing whistles. Everyone stopped and looked at Penny Harris.

"All the names are in this box," she announced. "We are going to pick four names and then go through some drills for a little while. At the end of the drills the captains are going to sit down and pick their players."

"This isn't going to work," Tasha muttered.

Before any of the Ballplayers had a chance to rise to Penny's defense, Sheila pushed through the crowd. She came to the front and said, "Sounds fair to me, P. Let's get this over with. I want to play!"

When Sheila spoke, even girls like Tasha fell in line. Sheila reached into the tissue box and pulled out the first name.

"The winner is . . ." She paused for suspense. "Phoebe!"

"Yes!" a few girls cheered. None of the Ballplayers objected. From what we knew of Phoebe, she was pretty cool and a solid athlete. Phoebe's eighth-grade friends reached out and gave her five. Sheila reached in and picked out another name.

"Behind door number two is . . ." She hesitated again. My nerves tingled. The thoughts of me being chosen as captain scared me. I was the youngest and smallest of the bunch. I hardly ever spoke and liked keeping my mouth shut. But then again, being captain was so cool. It gave you power and respect. I could pick a team instead of sweating through the draft.

"Helen Hart!" she called out with enthusiasm.

Helen grinned. My hopes started to slip away. The eighth graders were stealing the entire show. I didn't know Phoebe or Helen that well, but I knew they wouldn't pick a shorty. If one of the Ballplayers didn't get picked, I wouldn't have a shot at making a team. The moments between each pick seemed like forever. I waited for Sheila to reach back into the box. She mixed around the papers and stared up in the sky.

"Boring . . ." Tasha moaned.

Sheila pulled out the paper and shook her head.

"Who is it?" everyone asked.

"Trash-talking Tasha," Sheila said with a sigh.

Tasha threw her hands up in the air. I swallowed hard. Molly groaned. Penny whispered for her not to worry. Sheila reached in for the last name and the crowd held its breath. She pulled it out and grinned proudly. "Sweet P.!"

I jumped up and Molly cheered. Wil sighed in relief.

"This is fixed," one girl complained. I looked up and saw she was the same girl who had called me Shorty at school. Standing next to her was her sidekick, who had said that she almost couldn't see me. "This isn't fair," the girl whined. "Penny's always so lucky."

Shantell "Penny" Harris was nicknamed for good luck, and I felt her fortune. I tried to stay as close as possible to her in almost every drill. It wasn't because I needed protection or wanted to be her best friend like everyone else. Sweet P. would make me look like an All-pro on the field.

"Two lines over here," Wil hollered.

Wil called out the drills and explained them a few times. Nobody really listened at first. Everyone kind of made up things as they went along passing, catching, and throwing. But when it came to Penny's turn, everybody paid attention. The drills steadily improved, and Wil grinned proudly.

"We are big time, ladies!" she called out. "Kids are going to be reading about us in the history books someday!"

During the last few drills, fatigue set in. Girls started snapping at each other. Two-hand touch drills turned into two-arm push drills. I caught a ball on one play and felt Tasha's body slam into me. I hit the grass hard. Then she muttered, "Be careful, Shorty." I jumped back up and returned to the line. On the next play I shadowed Tasha and broke up the pass.

"You got lucky, Shorty," she muttered.

The two girls from school laughed at me. I glared at them both.

"You can't touch me," I mumbled.

"What?" one of the girls asked.

I said nothing.

"What did you say?" her friend barked.

The whistle blew and that was the end of the drills. We all collapsed on the ground and waited as Wil shuffled through her draft files. Papers and notes spilled out of her bag. She stuck a pen behind her ear and another one in her mouth.

"Give me just a second," she said, staring at her papers. "And then we'll be good to go."

Some girls whispered nervously as they stared around at the pool of players. I looked at Precious and Mookey, two cheerleaders who'd never seen a streak of dirt on their perfect skin. In every drill that I saw them in, they dropped the ball, missed the tackle, and threw like wimps. They sat quietly and waited. If I didn't get picked before them, I'd turn in my cleats and join the chess team. I turned to Molly and listened as she complained to Penny.

"Tasha had better not go breaking up the Ballplayers," Molly said. "And what about Helen? She might pick one of us to play on her team. I'm not playing if she does."

"You and Wil started this league," Penny said.

Penny caught my annoyed look.

"Oh, sorry," she said. "You, Wil, and Rosie thought of this. . . . Anyway, you can't quit now!"

Fear of being put on a team without friends seeped through the crowd. I guess all of us had assumed that captains would pick the girls they knew. But after the competitive drills and short tempers like Tasha's, it was clear that we were all playing to win.

"Who are you going to pick?" Molly asked Penny nervously.

Penny didn't answer.

"Try to get Sheila," Molly started. "She's good."

Penny nodded. "I bet Tasha is going to pick her up in the first round."

"Helen could go after Sheila, too," Molly added.

I looked away wondering whom Penny would pick.

Molly had me convinced that one captain was going to rock the boat and make things difficult for the rest of us. "Can we make trades?" I whispered to Molly.

"Hey, Wil," Molly called out. "Can captains trade players?"

"Yes," Wil announced.

"How many times?" Tasha asked.

"Well, um . . . I think just once," Wil said.

"That's not fair!" Tasha said.

"Can we just give this a shot, please?" Wil unloaded on Tasha. I don't blame Wil. She must have been up all night preparing the lists, schedule, and drills. I took a deep breath and sat back as the captains went up to the front of the group and took pens and notebooks. After a few seconds of their quiet conversations, a girl called out, "It's not polite to whisper!"

"Who's polite when they play football?" Molly yelled back.

The whole group began to grow restless.

"Let's go!"

"We don't have all day!"

"Is this the NFL or what?"

"Do we get any money if we get picked in the first round?"

I don't know who made the last comment, but everyone laughed. Wil announced the start of the first girls' football draft "in the glorious history of the United States of America."

"Call the president later," Tasha said. "Can we just get this over with? I've got a team to pick."

One by one each captain made her selection. Phoebe

picked her best friend, Kitty, who played like a lion that hadn't eaten in days. Helen chose her cousin, Betsy Miner, a bruiser who was also an arch rival of Molly's. Tasha went third, and she picked Sheila.

"How much money are you paying me?" Sheila joked.

"We'll talk contracts later," Wil announced. "It's your turn, P."

All eyes turned to Penny. Molly twisted her hands nervously and stared at the ground. If Penny didn't pick her, Molly would be devastated. If Penny didn't pick her other best friend, Wil would be brought to tears.

"I'll take Rosie," she said.

The crowd gasped in disbelief. Molly scoffed in disgust. Wil dropped her clipboard. I knew my friends weren't mad at me. They just wanted to be picked first by their friend. I didn't know what to think about everyone else. A girl giggled and said, "You picked Shorty?"

"I thought this was only for seventh and eighth graders," Tasha asked.

Penny smiled coolly. "Let's go to the second round."

Within seconds my suspicions and fear of the crowd's reaction wore off. I sat in awe. The coolest kid on the street had picked me first to be on her team.

"She only picked you because it was your idea to start the league and she didn't want to hurt Molly's and Wil's feelings," one girl said to me.

I didn't want to believe her. But in the second round Penny picked Mookey the cheerleader. My heart sank. I was convinced Penny felt bad for me and Mookey. That's why she picked us. I wanted to scream. By the third round the draft system bombed, and the whole league turned into one big cat fight over players, cheating and winning.

Penny whistled again. "If we don't work together," she said firmly, "people are going to say, 'They're just girls. They shouldn't play football anyway.'"

Her words hushed everyone. Even Tasha.

"Do you want that?" Penny called out.

"No," Molly mumbled.

"Do you want that?" Penny repeated louder.

A few girls yelled back, "No!"

"Then let's work together!"

"Why don't you just make the teams and see if the captains will agree on them?" Sheila suggested.

Penny waited for any objections.

"If that's what you want," she said. No one spoke. Penny took a look at her notebook and started writing. "Here it is," she said. "About twelve or thirteen players per team. I'm putting you all on teams based on where you live."

"We always do that," a girl whined. "Why don't you get some adults to run this?"

"If you don't like it, go home!" Wil snapped.

"I will!" the girl shot back. She got up and left.

"Anybody else?" Penny asked.

Nobody moved.

"Each team is responsible for finding a coach and proper equipment," Wil announced.

Penny read off the list of teams and their respective captains.

"Huddle together for a few minutes," Wil added. "First

game is next weekend. The rules will be posted in the girls' bathrooms."

I ended up back on Penny's team. When the Ballplayers and I got together for our first team meeting, all I could do was stare at Mookey and Precious as they walked over to us.

"Why'd you pick them?" Molly asked. "They're cheerleaders. I don't think they understand that they're actually going to have to wear smelly uniforms."

"Everybody has to play," Penny said. "Those are the rules."

"All right, fine. But why'd you pick them before me?" Molly asked. "Am I that bad?"

Penny didn't answer because Precious and Mookey were in earshot. They had to know people were talking about them. Even I knew that people were still talking about me. I couldn't look anyone else in the eye for the rest of the day. Penny picked me because she knew no one else would want a shorty.

Chapter Six

I pushed open the front door, walked across the living room, and flopped down on the couch.

"Get up!" my mother yelled from the kitchen. "And get those cleats off!"

I stared down at the floor, not wanting to cooperate until I saw the lumps of dirt that I had trailed across the carpet.

"Rosa!" my mother screamed. *"Mira lo que has hecho ahora, muchacha! Limpia eso!"*

I wanted to tell her all about my awful experience at football practice, but now didn't seem like it was a good time to feel sorry for myself. I slid off my shoes, set them down by the door, and kept my eyes on the paper towel rack as I walked across the kitchen.

"Porqué haces estas cosas?" she muttered. *"Estas*

loco? La juventud de hoy no piensa."

She was accusing me of being young and not thinking. But that was not important. When she spoke in Spanish for a long period of time, I knew she was close to flying off the handle and doing something crazy like grounding me for a month. I quickly cleaned up my mud trail and ran into my room. After I put on a clean T-shirt and sweatpants, I returned to my favorite spot on the living room couch.

"No more television!" my mother called out. "Do some homework!"

"It's Friday night, Ma," I said.

"I don't care!" she snapped. "Read! Do what Miss Lopez says!"

She hustled across the room and switched the television off. I stared at her as she held her frown. My mother's long brown hair slid out of her bun. The dark lines under her eyes and sharp tone of her voice made me nervous.

"What's the matter, Ma?" I asked.

"Nothing," she said. "Go and read in your room until dinner is ready."

"Is Rico coming home?" I asked as I stood up.

"I don't know," my mother said.

I went into my room, picked up a magazine, and read an article on Olympic fastpitch softball star Lisa Fernandez for the twelfth time. A lot of coaches and parents talked about me switching from baseball to softball, but I didn't think I could make it without playing my favorite sport with my brother. Rico never held anything against softball nor did he ever tell me not to play. My dad said playing with the boys made me better. Of course my mother said she'd go to any game I played in, but also mentioned that a lot of girls get softball scholarships to college. Whenever the issue of college came up, the conversation always turned back to Rico and his mistakes.

I heard a gentle rap on the door. I smiled, knowing it was Rico. I quickly opened my Roberto Clemente baseball book and stuck my nose in it.

"Come in!" I yelled.

"Hey, kid," he said with a grin. "How'd football practice go today?"

"Fine." I stared back at my book. "You staying for dinner?"

He nodded and then eyed me suspiciously. "What's wrong, kid?" he asked as he tapped my cap down over my nose. "You don't seem very excited about football anymore. What happened?"

"Nothing," I muttered. "You're still coaching us, right?"

"Yeah, If you want me to." Then my brother paused. "Well, do you?"

I nodded. "We have practice Sunday afternoon at the park," I told him.

"I'm not going to go unless you tell me what's buggin' you," he said with a grin. I wasn't in the mood for playing games. I set my book down on the bed and huffed.

"We had a draft," I said. "Penny picked me first."

"That's good," he said.

"No, it's not," I told him. "She only picked me because she knew all the other older kids wouldn't pick me at all.

I'm 'Shorty.' I'm the one who they never think is big enough to play."

He smiled at me.

"It's not funny!" I said. "Being little is not cute any-more! It never was!"

"Don't worry, kid," he said. "You're faster and you're smarter than all of them."

"Try telling Dad I'm smart," I said. "He's always bug-ging me about reading and school. He even has Mom all over my case. And it gets worse—now my teacher, Miss Lopez, is making me do all this extra homework."

"That's just Dad being Dad," Rico said.

I huffed and rolled my eyes. Dad being Dad was not an acceptable explanation. I needed some sympathy here.

"Have you heard anything else about moving?" I asked.

Rico shook his head. My mother called out for us to come to the table. When my brother slowly stood up and stretched his stiff legs, I could see today had been a weight-lifting day. He massaged his right shoulder with his left hand and then rotated it around in his socket. Baseball and Broadway Ave. were our lives. "We're not moving anywhere, kid," Rico assured me.

We walked into the kitchen and sat down at the table. Within a few minutes our father joined us.

"How'd practice go?" he asked.

"Fine," I replied.

"Are you drinking a lot of milk and eating right?" he asked me.

I looked down at my plate, "Yeah."

"You'll need strong bones and a lot of energy to score touchdowns."

I braced myself for another lecture on nutrition and vitamins. I wondered if he was going to pull out a scale and start weighing me in.

"Eat your spinach and you'll be an all-pro," he added with a smile. He scooped an extra helping of mushy dark green spinach on my plate. I groaned. Spinach tasted like slimy dirt to me. I looked at Rico for sympathy. *It's just Dad being Dad.* He raised his eyebrow and shrugged.

"Are you playing football with enough protective gear?" my mother asked.

"Pads, Ma," I said. "Yes, we're playing with helmets and shoulder pads."

She blinked twice and I watched the muscles in her neck tighten. She hummed as she walked back to the oven, which was a clear sign that she was not happy about something.

"What's wrong, Ma?" Rico asked.

"I just don't like this football idea at all," she said.

"We have a chance to be the first girls' league in history," I said.

"Are you sure about that?" my dad asked. "I think I read in the paper a story about a team in Minnesota?"

"We haven't heard about it," I muttered.

All of us made it through dinner with small talk. Just as we finished, my father announced that he was glad we all had a moment to be together.

"I have something I need to tell you," he said.

I gripped the bottom of my chair tight. I stared at Rico. He ignored me and kept his serious eyes on my father. My mother wiped the corners of her mouth and looked at me with sad eyes. I turned to my father. He spoke without looking at any of us.

"I've decided that it would be best for our family and for me to take this new position in my company," he said. "The only difficult part about this decision is that we will have to move."

I couldn't speak. I kept blinking and shaking my head.

"What?" Rico said. "Are you serious?"

My father nodded. "I was hoping that you would support me for once."

Rico shook his head in disgust. "It's not that we're not supporting you. You just go making all the decisions by yourself."

"I am one of the people running this family, which means I make the decisions around here!" my father said.

"How can you let him do this?" I asked my mother. Then I turned my fury back to my father. "You make *all* the decisions! You never let her do anything!"

My father ignored our pleas. He sat there and quietly gave out instructions. "We have to sell the house first," he began. "We're going to have an open house on Sunday."

"Are you sure about this?" Rico asked. "Is it really going to happen?"

"I'm ninety-nine percent sure," he said. "I'm just waiting for my boss to give me the green light."

"You may get the green light, but I'm not going anywhere!" I yelled.

I stormed off to my room and slammed the door behind me.

Chapter Seven

I called Sleepy first thing the next morning. Instead of talking about my life being turned upside down, all I wanted to do was play ball. Sleepy agreed to go to the park. He even said he'd stop over to pick me up. I smiled in relief as I hung up the phone. He sounded like good ol' Sleepy.

While I waited for my best friend, my father passed me in the living room. "What are you doing today?" he asked.

I shrugged. What right did he have to ask about my life when he told us nothing?

"It's a nice day to go to the cages and work on your swing," he said.

I didn't say anything. He told me that he'd be back later and headed out the door. I watched him as he walked down the driveway and opened the back car door. He rested his briefcase on the backseat and then opened the driver's side. That briefcase had to be filled with houses that I would never live in.

Out of the corner of my eye, I noticed someone running across my front lawn. I turned and saw Sleepy as he flipped his cap backward just like Rico and I always did. As I rushed out the front door, I pushed my fears of moving down deep inside of me. I did not leak a word to my best friend or to any of the Ballplayers, who joined us at the park for a full day of sports and fun.

"You've got a lot of energy today," Sleepy said to me as we shot hoops.

If I kept moving, no one would have a chance to ask me to confirm any possible rumors. I picked up a basketball and dribbled the full length of the court.

"You're making me tired just watching you," Wil added.

Just when I thought there was no need to worry, I looked up and squinted down the street. Pete the Creep pulled up on his handlebars and popped a wheelie all the way down the street.

"Here comes Pea Brain," Wil said.

I looked at Sleepy and watched as he joked around with Beef Potato and J. J. He was around boys who were on most days fair to him and fair to us. A kid like Pete didn't belong on Broadway Ave. If I was a talker like Molly, I would have said something. All I did was hope he would ride away.

Penny called out the start of the next game. Out of the corner of my eye, I clocked every move Pete made.

When he rode past the courts, I breathed a huge sigh of relief.

Later on, as Sleepy and I walked home, Molly called out for me. "Don't forget about practice tomorrow," she said.

I nodded.

"Is Rico coaching?" she asked.

I nodded again.

"My dad is bringing a bunch of equipment," she said.

"See you tomorrow," I said as I jogged to catch up with my best friend.

"I'll race you to the stop sign?" Sleepy offered.

"Let me say 'go,'" I agreed quickly.

"Ready, set . . ."

As usual, we never followed the "go" rule. Taking off early, we both reached the stop sign, matching strides.

"I won," I said.

"Keep dreaming," Sleepy huffed.

We both bent over in fatigue. I closed my eyes and then opened them when I heard a creepy voice.

"Hey, Sleepy," Pete called out as he zipped by us on his bike. "Can she beat you in everything?"

Sleepy grimaced as he bent over and picked up the largest rock he could find. He wound up and flung his arm forward, but held the rock clenched in his hand. Pete's eyes grew wide. He swerved as he tried to speed away. His tire jackknifed and he hit the pavement. He jumped back up with a beet-red face and hopped back on his bike. Pete the Creep had gotten what he deserved.

But my conversation with Sleepy grew weaker as we walked. My mind recalled what Pete had said. Sleepy had to have been thinking about it, too.

"Hey," Sleepy said as we walked closer to our house. "What's that sign doing on your front lawn?"

I looked up and spotted a green-and-white sign that read:

> ## For Sale
> ## Open House
> ## Sunday 2 p.m.—4 p.m.

"It's nothing," I said.

"What do you mean, it's nothing?" he asked.

I thought of telling him that it seemed like some kind of mistake or prank. The Ballplayers and I liked to move people's lawn ornaments around the neighborhood for fun. But there was something about this sign and how it was planted where everyone could see it that made it seem too real for me to even try and make up a lie.

"Are you moving?" Sleepy gasped.

I did not respond.

"Is it for real?" he asked again.

"Maybe my family is moving," I said. "But I'm not."

As we walked up to my driveway, I marched right up to the sign, pulled it out of the dirt, and threw it on the ground.

Sleepy's eyes grew wide.

"What?" I asked defensively.

"I'm outta here when your dad sees what you just did," he said.

"If he puts it back up, I'm taking it down again later,"

I told him. "You're going to help me, right?"

"What?" Sleepy gasped.

I paused for a moment to put together my master plan. "If you look out and see the sign up before you go to bed, set your alarm for one A.M."

"Why?" he asked.

"I'm going to go outside and knock it down again," I explained.

"Why do you need me?" he asked.

I huffed in frustration. This was just another sign of our struggling relationship. "You don't want me running around at night by myself, do you?" I asked.

"No," he said. "But the sign is right outside your door. Why do you need me?"

I stood silently, hoping for some kind of appreciation and support.

"Are you scared?" he asked.

"No, I'm not scared!" I shot back. "I just thought you'd stand behind me on this one."

A moment of silence passed. Sleepy's droopy eyes turned away.

"You probably don't even care if I move away or not," I muttered.

Sleepy scoffed in disgust. "I can't believe you just said that," he said.

I felt bad about delivering the low blow, but I didn't take it back. We went our separate ways without speaking again.

When my father returned home later that night, I watched him stop in front of the sign and stick it back in the ground. He threw his weight behind his push and the sign sank deep into the dirt. I went into my brother's bedroom and watched a baseball movie by myself.

I could not fall asleep that night. I went back and forth reading magazines, organizing my baseball cards, and tossing the ball in and out of my mitt. I checked the clock every few minutes. When it read 12:55 A.M., I put phase one of Operation I'm Not Moving into action. Exiting out of my bedroom door was not a possibility. My mother, who slept with her eyes and her door both half-open, would surely catch me. I flipped on my flashlight and directed it at my window.

Adrenaline rushed through me as I tiptoed across the room. I gently flicked the latch and held my breath as I slid the window up. I grabbed the notches on the screen and winced as the metal clips pinched my fingers. I pulled tighter. *Click.* Slowly I slid the screen up. *Click. Click.* I flipped my garbage can over and took one step up. I tugged on the rope that I had tied to my bed and then tossed the rope into the cold fall air. I hopped up on the ledge and flipped my body around so I could climb down our brick house. The air escaped my lungs, and my insides ached as I slid down the hard, rough wall. I felt for the garden hose with my foot and finally tapped it gently as I hung from the rope. One false move would make the water gush out the spout. My mom would hear the pump, and she'd call the police. I pressed to the left of the handle and felt it twist tight. I pushed off the brick wall. Both feet quietly landed on the ground together. I wished Rico had seen me stick the landing.

I sprinted across the lawn in the chilly darkness. I

stopped in front of the sign, reached out, and tugged with all my might.

"Hey," I heard a voice whisper.

I dropped down behind the sign.

"You look like you need some help," Sleepy said.

I peeked around the sign and slowly stood up.

"Thanks," I said as he tightly gripped the sign. We counted to three quietly and then removed the sign from the ground.

"What should we do with it?" I asked.

"I don't know," Sleepy said. "I've got to go home."

He started to panic. I felt every second tick.

"Leave it here," Sleepy said.

"What if I throw it out?" I asked.

"What if he catches you?"

"I don't care," I snapped.

"You should have thought of that a little sooner," he said. "Come on, Rosie. We'd better get back inside."

I gently lowered the sign to the ground and whispered "thanks" to my best friend. We both took off without saying good-bye. I heard Sleepy stop running as I stepped on the tap and clenched the rope. Once I had made it to the window, Sleepy took off again.

My father slept in the next morning. Rico was out with Natalie all night. The only person I had to deal with was my mother. She ordered me around the house with things to do.

"I don't like to have to make you do this," she said. "But I need some help."

I took my time cleaning up around the place.

"This place looks fine," I said.

"Please, Rosa," she asked.

I did as little as I could. Then she told me to get ready for church.

"Church?" I asked.

"Yes," she said. "The place we go on Sunday mornings."

I didn't appreciate her sarcasm, yet didn't take time to respond. All I could think of was not letting her see that sign. She'd report to my father, and he'd put it up again. I rushed into my room and stared out the window. I eyed the distance between the sign and the driveway, and then anticipated which way she would turn down Broadway. With a little traffic and a lot of talk, she could easily be distracted.

The second phase of Operation I'm Not Moving ran as smoothly as my brother's fastball. But the ride home from church posed a much greater challenge. I tried talking loudly about how much homework I had done for Miss Lopez in the past week. I stared at my mother's eyes as she turned the wheel. She looked off to the right with a frown. When she didn't see the sign, her brow furrowed. She looked to the ground. "The sign is down."

"Must be the wind," I said. "It was really blowing like crazy last night."

"It was?" my mother asked. "I didn't hear anything."

The first thing my mother did when we walked into the front door was report to my father the news about the sign being facedown on the ground.

"That's strange," my father said. "Was there a storm last night?"

"No," my mother said as she shrugged. "But I guess it was really windy."

As my father walked outside to return the sign to its upright position, he muttered something about the "rotten kids in the neighborhood." I wanted to scream in protest, but I couldn't blow my cover. As he left, I stared at my mother.

"Why'd you tell him about the sign being down?" I asked. "Do you want us to move, too?"

"Rosalinda," she said patiently. "How many times do I have to explain this to you?"

Just that moment Rico walked through the front door with a big smile on his face. "It's a perfect day for some football!"

My mother moaned. "Oh, you're not really playing, are you?" she asked me.

"Yep," I said proudly. It felt good to do something my parents didn't want me to do. "Today is our first practice," I added.

At that moment it occurred to me that my father had this all planned. The open house was during the same time we had practice at the park. He wanted me out of the picture because he knew I would be miserable. The phone rang and I jumped to it. I heard the voice of that Frank guy who had called earlier in the week about the houses. He asked for my father.

"No, he's not here right now," I said.

"Is your mother home?" he asked.

I stared at my mother as she dusted the living room for the third time in less than twenty-four hours.

"She's not here either," I lied.

"Please tell them that Frank called," he said.

"Okay," I said. "Bye."

I hung up the phone and looked up at my mother, who stood with her hand on her hip. "Who was that?" she asked.

"Somebody trying to sell something," I said.

A little later in the afternoon I talked Rico into leaving a few minutes early for practice. He said to go wait in the car and that he'd be right out. I rushed outside and took one last look at the ugly green-and-white sign. I looked to my right and left. Then I ran up to our front window and cupped my hands around my eyes. I leaned against it and looked inside. My mother and father were in the kitchen. They had their backs turned to me.

In a wild fury I sprinted out to the sign and yanked it out of the dirt. I pulled so hard that I fell on the ground. I jumped up and ran with it over my head down the alley. The muscles in my arms burned. I grunted as I focused on Mr. Miller's garbage cans. He was an old man living alone. He didn't have to empty the trash for at least another two or three days. He wouldn't notice an ugly green sign in his alley. I turned the sign so the writing was facing the fence. I tried to set it down gently, but it slipped. *Bang!* My heart skipped a beat. I raced back down the alley, turned down the sidewalk on the side of my house, and stopped right in front of Rico.

"What are you doing?" he asked seriously.

"Warming up," I said. "Are you ready to go?"

"Sure, kid," he said.

My nerves tingled. I rushed to my door and hoped Rico would hurry up and roll the getaway car out of the driveway.

Chapter Eight

The damp smell of leaves, grass, and mud filled the air at Anderson Park. I sprinted across the field ahead of my brother and stopped in front of the Ballplayers. Wil pulled a pencil off her ear and stared down at rows and piles of equipment. Then she scratched down check marks on her clipboard.

"Looks like I'm not going to have to write to the NFL after all," she announced proudly. "We've got everything we need."

Penny knocked over the neat pile of mud-stained pants.

"Hey!" Wil said.

"Sorry," Penny mumbled. Then she picked up two old helmets. "They could use some paint."

"We're all going to get dirty anyway," Molly added. "Who cares?"

Mr. Harris, Rico, and Mr. O'Malley walked over to our huddle and hustled us out on the field. "Warm up, girls!" Mr. O. said.

We jogged out to join the rest of our teammates. I looked around the park hoping to see Miss Lopez. As we took the field, Wil said, "Do you think we have enough coaches?"

I wanted so badly to tell them that Miss Lopez was on her way, but the way the week was going, I had a bad feeling that Miss Lopez didn't care about me, either.

"Who's coaching the other teams?"

"Who cares?" Molly scoffed.

As usual Penny always thought about others; Molly always thought about winning; and Wil thought about everything. Angel walked up along the sideline. She had her hair pulled back in a blue bow. We threw her a few passes, and Penny cracked some jokes. I could tell by Angel's careful steps that her feet were in pain.

"You still using those potatoes on your dawgs?" Wil called out.

Angel shook her head.

"I'm telling you—it works if you stick with the treatment long enough," Wil advised.

Wil had passed along an old wives' tale about how taping potatoes to the bottoms of sore feet would soak the pain out of them. "I'm thinkin' of using the potatoes all over my body after our football games," she said.

The whistle blew and we all jogged over to our coaches.

"Hey, Rosie," Molly whispered. "Is Miss Lopez coming?"

I hesitated a moment, trying to think of some excuse

70

to cover for my teacher and not give up on hope. "I think she had something else to do today," I said. "But maybe on Thursday she'll be here."

Molly nodded. Her serious blue eyes turned to her dad.

"Two lines of jogs, sprints, and then monkey rolls," he announced.

"Monkey rolls?" Wil gasped. "What are they?"

All three coaches smiled broadly. They lined up next to each other. Rico dropped and rolled along the grass to his right. Mr. Harris jumped over him and then dropped and rolled. Rico jumped up and Mr. O'Malley waited for Mr. Harris to come rolling under him. Molly's dad jumped up but not high enough. He tripped over the other man's shoulder and hit the ground.

Our entire team was bent over laughing.

"Stop before we have to call the ambulance!" Penny yelled.

"Those monkey rolls are not cool," Wil said.

"It's not that bad," Molly said.

"Let's give it a shot, girls," Mr. O. cheered. "You don't want people saying you're not tough enough."

One by one we glared at our coaches as we lined up to beat our bodies against the ground. Within seconds we burst into painful laughter, moans, and groans. "I've had enough!" Wil said firmly. "Can we go to bear crawls now?"

Mr. Harris blew the whistle and granted Wil her wish. As the coaches set us into our bear crawls and footwork drills, Mookey and Precious jogged up to the field. Mookey pulled her ponytail high on her head and tightened her pink bow. Precious wore a tight lavender sweatsuit.

"Sorry we're late, P.," Mookey whispered.

"Probably came from cheerleading practice," Molly muttered.

"That's all right, Mook," Penny said, ignoring Molly. "Jump in line."

Molly looked at me and rolled her eyes. "I don't know why they're even here."

The coaches blew the whistle and switched to skill drills. I stepped up in the passing line. I glanced over to my partner, Anita, who stood a full head and shoulders above me. She rolled her eyes as she looked at me. Anita always dreaded keeping up with shorties like me. Even though we were friends, my nerves tingled in excitement as I thought about using my size and speed to make me a bigger threat than the tallest person on the field. I turned to my brother, and he winked. Mr. O'Malley said "Go!" He hiked the ball to himself. I ran straight and then peeled to the right. It didn't even feel like my feet were hitting the ground. Mr. O. drilled the ball right at me. I reached out and felt the pigskin stick to my hands. I tucked it in and burned Anita down the sideline.

"Atta way, kid!" my brother yelled.

Anita tripped, gasped, and grunted. I turned to her and said, "Way to hustle, 'Nita."

She winced. "I wish I had your feet."

All of us raced through drills except for Mookey and Precious, who tiptoed through their routes and dropped easy passes. They barely made contact with anybody on the defensive drills. Penny tried to cheer them through each dreadful play. Everybody else mumbled words of doubt under their breath.

"They're not even trying," Molly said.

"Somebody tell them that it's okay to touch people in football," Wil added.

The coaches huddled us together and announced the rules about pads and helmets. Rico and Mr. O. handed out all the equipment as Mr. Harris spoke. I put on a huge pair of pants and stuffed the pads inside. Everybody laughed when they saw that I could pull the pants all the way up to my neck.

"You could fit three of you in there," Jen joked.

My brother tucked my blue jersey in and weaved a belt through the loopholes in the pants and tied the belt tight around my chest. My nerves tingled as I thought about putting on the helmet. We all smiled as we twisted our heads and pulled the hard hat on tight.

"This is awesome!" Molly yelled.

Then we started jogging. I felt like I was stuck in a wet snowsuit. Others were talking, laughing, and complaining. Wil started shouting.

"This feels funny," she said. "Doesn't it?"

"I feel like I'm an astronaut," Molly added. "This is cool."

I gazed up at Anita, who looked as big as a refrigerator.

"I look pretty dumb, don't I?" she asked.

"No," I said. "Just really, really strong."

My arms felt heavy and stiff in the shoulder pads. When I muffed a few catches during the drills, the coaches said to shake it off. "You'll need a little time to adjust with those pads on," Mr. Harris said.

On the last play of the day Penny dashed through the whole defensive line and streaked down the entire field. At the end she just coolly dropped the football.

"Spike it next time!" Molly said.

"Do a dance or do something like this!" Wil added.

All eyes turned to Wil as she started swimming in place. Then she held her nose and wiggled down to the ground. Everybody started laughing, including the coaches.

"You'd better save that swimming stuff for the pool," Penny said.

"I'm just having a little fun," Wil said with a big grin. "Our football league is going to be the talk of the city."

"Let's celebrate after our first W.," Penny said.

"We will," Wil agreed surely. "Count on it!"

After practice Rico waved goodbye to me.

"Wait!" I called out. He couldn't leave. I wanted a few moments to talk strategy, players, positions, and the potential of our team. "Where are you going?"

He waved, smiled, and said, "I'm late. See ya later, kid!" Then he ducked into his car and rushed off to Natalie's. Frustration ran from head to toe. I had to find a way to get Miss Lopez at practice.

"Are you walking home?" Wil asked me.

I nodded.

"Let's go," she said. "I'm tired."

I listened to Wil babble the whole way home and loved every minute of it. "We're one game a week for the next two weeks, then a round-robin tournament— you know what that is, right? When you play each team and keep track of wins and points."

I nodded.

"Then we're matching the two top teams up for the championship," she announced. "I've got to get a huge trophy for the winners. You think your big bro can hook us up with somebody who makes trophies? He has enough of them."

I nodded again. Rico hadn't officially made it as a major leaguer in baseball yet, but on Broadway, the kids had considered him an all-pro ever since he starred in high school.

Wil turned toward her building. I waved goodbye and then kept walking to my house. I was relieved that Wil didn't ask me anything about moving. With the sign hidden in Mr. Miller's alley, I was sure nobody had showed up at our house that day.

I walked up the driveway and a shot of fear almost knocked me over. The green-and-white sign stood tall in our front lawn. Two wooden posts buttressed its sides. I looked at my front door and did not move. I considered running away from home. Living in an apartment with Rico was another possibility.

The front door creaked open and I jumped. My mother looked at me with a steely glare that pulled me up the driveway and into my house. My father sat in the living room chair and waited for me to take off my shoes.

"Have a seat," he said.

I plopped down on the couch.

"Sit up straight," my mother said.

"Do you know anything about the sign that keeps disappearing?" my father asked.

I shook my head.

"Are you sure?"

I said nothing. My muscles grew tight. I hid my eyes under the bill of my cap.

"Mr. Miller said a short girl with a long braid dumped that sign in his trash," he said. "You wouldn't happen to know anyone who fits that description?"

I did not say a word. Wil always told us to take the Fifth Amendment of the Constitution in these kinds of pressure situations. I absolutely refused to incriminate myself.

"Frank said that he called twice this week," my father added. "I never got the messages."

"Do you have anything to say?" my mother asked.

"Yeah," I said. "This isn't fair. I'm not moving!"

"One more stunt and you'll be off the football team," my father said firmly. "Go to your room."

I walked down the hallway and ducked into Rico's room. I held my breath, hoping that my mother hadn't seen me. I picked up the phone and dialed Sleepy's number. He answered.

"Can I move in with you?" I asked.

"What?"

"I'm serious, Sleep."

"Did you get caught?" he asked.

"Kind of."

Sleepy clicked his tongue. "I told you."

"Come on, please."

"I don't know," he said. "We don't have a lot of room over here."

"Think about it."

"How was football practice?" he asked.

"Fine," I said slowly, curious about why he changed the subject so quickly.

"Is your team any good?" he asked.

I didn't like the tone of his voice. He knew most of my teammates. He knew we could play. "Yeah," I said suspiciously. "Why?"

"I was just wondering."

"The boys are talking like we're not good enough, aren't they?" I asked.

"No," he said. "Not really."

Before I could say any more, my mother appeared in the door. I stood upright.

"Thanks for the help on the homework," I said to Sleepy.

"What?" he said.

"See you at school tomorrow," I added nervously. *Click.*

My mother walked into the room, pressed her finger on the button and removed the phone from my hand. "Sounds like you have a lot of homework," she said.

I nodded as my eyes shifted around the room. I jumped up to flee the situation, but a firm hand gripped my shoulder.

"Please understand how difficult this is on all of us," she said. I looked up and saw a tear in her eye.

The phone rang. I stared at it. My mother picked it up and said hello.

"Hi, Penny," my mother said. "Rosa cannot come to the phone right now."

"Please can I talk to her?" I begged. "Just for one sec-

ond. I promise I won't touch the sign. I'll do my homework."

My mother huffed and said, "Hold on a minute." She
rested the phone against her shoulder. "You've got ten
seconds." She handed me the receiver.

"Hey," Penny said. "I saw a sign on your front lawn. Is
everything all right?"

"Umm," I said.

"Are you moving?" she asked.

"No," I said.

"Then what is that sign doing on your front lawn?"
Penny asked.

I didn't answer.

"Rosie?"

I remained silent.

"Do you want to talk about this later?" she asked.

"Uh-huh," was all I could manage.

"Do you want me to say anything to the kids on
Broadway?"

"No," I said.

"What if they ask?" Penny said.

Again, I had no desire or energy to reply.

Before hanging up, Penny said, "Hang in there, Ro.
We're behind you."

Chapter Nine

After getting only about six hours of sleep Sunday night, I was a girl of even fewer words the next morning at school. My best friend didn't bug me about talking. He merely gave me some simple questions.

"Did you do your math homework?" Sleepy asked.

I shook my head.

"Science?" he asked as he looked closer at me.

"Nope," I said.

His eyes grew wide. "English?"

"Uh-uh," I muttered.

I threw my books into my locker and yawned.

"Miss Lopez is going to be all over your case," Sleepy said.

"So?" I said. "I'm mad at her anyway."

"Why?" he asked.

"She didn't come to our football practice yesterday."

"Was she supposed to?" Sleepy asked.

I hesitated. "Yeah. She knew about it."

"Let's go, you two!" Mr. Gordon's voice boomed. "Off to class!"

As Mr. G. stormed down the hallway, kids scattered like a flock of birds. I went to math class. When my teacher asked us to hand up the homework, I untied and then tied my sneaker. In science class, I asked to use the rest room when our class went over our assignment. All my mind could think about was moving and football.

"Did you get in trouble?" Sleepy asked me as I walked to the lunchroom later that morning.

I shook my head. "None of my teachers noticed."

"Wait till tomorrow," he said.

"I'll hand it all in by then," I assured him.

"What are you going to do about Miss Lopez?"

"She won't care," I muttered.

"Yeah, right," he added. "You'd better think of something."

I tossed my brown lunch bag on the table and sat with the Ballplayers as Sleepy went over to eat with the boys from Broadway. Penny flashed me a sympathetic smile. I mumbled "hey" to everyone and sat down on the bench.

Wil eyed me suspiciously as she bit into her peanut butter and jelly sandwich. "You all right, Ro?"

"Just tired," I said.

"Losing sleep over something?" Molly asked.

My eyes darted to Penny. She shrugged. "I had to tell them," she admitted. "I'm sorry if you're mad. But we're all worried."

"Are you really moving?" Wil asked.

I shrugged.

"When?" Molly asked.

I took a sip of milk.

"You're killing me!" Wil screamed. "Talk to us, please!"

"My family might be moving, but I'm not."

"What?" Molly asked.

"I'm not going," I said. "I told them already. I'll convince Rico to get an apartment, and I'll move in with him."

Silence fell upon our table.

"Is there anything we can do?" Penny asked.

I thought of possible positions they could take in Operation I'm Not Moving.

"We could tell everyone that your house is haunted," Wil suggested. "I can make up some really good scary stories."

I nodded. It was worth a shot.

"All you have to do is go along with what I say and add a little more each time," Wil said. "Like if people ask if you saw the spirits out your window, you say you saw a mother, grandmother, and great-grandmother of spirits dancing with angels and singing Puerto Rican songs."

Molly's brow furrowed. She shook her head at Wil. "You're really strange, do you know that?"

"Eccentric," Wil said. "I am definitely eccentric."

"Nobody is going to believe the ghost stories," Penny said.

"How about making your roof leak or bringing in some bugs," Molly suggested.

"Gross," I said.

"You don't actually make your ceiling leak," she said. "Just maybe you put a whole bunch of buckets around the floors so it looks like you have a dumpy house."

"My mother would scream," I told her.

I appreciated my friends' support, but didn't want to get them too involved. My father was already mad enough. As we finished lunch, Eddie and J. J. started throwing spitballs at us. One bounced off Wil's cheek.

"Don't even tell me that Eddie's slime just touched my beautiful skin," she said.

I laughed.

"That's it!" Wil said as she ripped open my milk carton and dabbed a napkin in it. "It's on!"

She looked over both her shoulders to make sure the lunchroom monitors were looking the other way. She squeezed the chocolate milk ball in her hand. Then she handed it to me.

"What?" I said.

"You've got the better arm," she said. "Hit Eddie right between the eyes for me. Maybe it will knock some sense into him."

I glanced at the lunch monitors again. Molly and Penny giggled as they sat up straight to hide me from any witnesses. I stayed low against the table and cocked my arm back. Just as Eddie turned to look at me, the wad of wet milk slapped him right on the nose. Our whole table erupted in laughter.

"You think we're tough now," Wil said. "Wait until you see us play football on Sunday."

"We're not going to your stupid football game," Eddie said.

Pete's scrawny little head popped up behind the huddle of boys. "You girls are so weak."

"I want to pancake him," Molly said to us. "I should have brought my pads to school and mowed him down in the hallway just once. He'd never mess with us again."

"I told you," Pete said. "Girls can't play."

I grabbed Wil's last napkin, dipped it deep into my carton, and squeezed. My arm whipped back furiously. Right after Pete said "football" my milky bullet smacked him square in his big forehead. Both tables exploded in laughter as the milk dripped down his face.

My moment of glory kept me smiling until I walked into Miss Lopez's classroom later that day. She stood right in front of my desk and asked everyone to hand in their homework. She put out her hand and stared down at me. I looked up and twiddled my thumbs.

"Well?" she asked. "Where's your work?"

I shrugged.

"Out in the hallway right now!" she said firmly.

All the other kids in the class froze and looked at me in fear. I had never been chewed out in the hallway before. But from what I heard, Miss Lopez sometimes yelled so loud that the other teachers closed their doors. I slowly dragged myself out of my desk and followed my teacher. She sprinted to the doorway with her fists clenched. The kids in my class winced. I rolled my eyes and acted as if I didn't care at all.

"You'd better start talking, young lady!" she said.

She squinted her brown eyes. I stared right back at her, but said nothing.

"What's the matter with you?" she asked.

"What's the matter with you?" I shot back.

She flinched. "Don't talk to me that way!"

"You didn't come to our football practice yesterday," I said.

"I told you I already had plans," she said.

I clicked my tongue and mumbled, "Whatever." I regretted saying everything right at that instant. Miss Lopez's face turned so red I didn't know whether she was going to burst into tears or set a record for the loudest voice in Lincoln School.

"I'm sorry," I said. "I'll hand in my homework tomorrow."

"I'm calling your father," she said.

"He doesn't care about me anyway," I told her.

"What do you mean by that?"

"Ask him," I said. "Ask him why he's planning on selling our house—just so he can have a better life. He doesn't care about me or my brother or my mom."

Miss Lopez stood up straight and folded her arms. "So that's what this is all about," she said, cooling off. "You're moving?"

"I'm not moving," I said stubbornly.

"Back in the room," she said as she touched my shoulder and turned me around. "We'll talk about this later."

"Wait," I said as I spun around. "I'm still mad at you."

She sighed and dropped her chin down. "If you hand in all your homework and don't ever bring your lousy attitude or smart mouth back in my classroom, I'll reconsider our friendship," she said.

"What about coaching?" I asked.

"Let's take one thing at a time."

Chapter Ten

Although I was still miserable about the thought of moving, I didn't take any chances with my schoolwork. I handed in every boring assignment. Fearing that any one of my teachers might spill the beans about my previous week's performance, I dodged Mr. Gordon successfully three times at school on Monday and Tuesday. On Wednesday my luck ran out. He stepped outside a classroom and right in front of me.

"Well, Miss Jones," he said. "How many A's have you received this week?

"Ummm," I muttered nervously. "Three, I think."

"Very nice," he said. "And how's Miss Lopez's class?"

My eyes shifted around the hallway. "Fine," I said quickly.

Before another second passed I had to change the

subject. "Did you hear about our football league?"

"I sure did," his voice bellowed. "I'll be there on Sunday for your first game."

As Mr. Gordon created a path down the hallway, I grinned. The whole school had heard about "the League" as Wil called it.

"Why call it anything else?" she had said. "It's the one and only."

The list of rules and regulations were posted in the bathroom stalls:

THE LEAGUE RULES!

1. Full pads.
2. No crying.
3. No whining.

LEAGUE SLOGAN: HEART AND GUTS!

J. J. scanned over a list of the rules and shook his head as he stopped in front of the Ballplayers. "What is this doing in the boys' bathroom?"

"Just wanted to show you how all games should be played," Wil added.

Pete the Creep popped his skinny head up in the crowd.

"We want a game against you," he said.

"Get outta town, Pete," Penny said. "Not a chance."

"Why not?" he asked. "Are you scared?"

"We've got nothin' to prove," Molly said.

As a pack, we all moved away from the boys. I felt taller and stronger with every step.

Wil broke from our group and darted from locker to locker handing out flyers to kids. "See you Sunday!" she said.

"Wil," Molly said. "It's Wednesday. What are you doing?"

"There's plenty of promotional material to go around all week," she insisted.

When we reached the lunchroom, the noise of hungry kids stole our thunder. After splitting up into different lunch lines, we all met a few minutes later and sat down at our table.

"What's the latest on your house, Ro?" Molly asked.

I shrugged and chewed the food in my mouth. "I told you," I said as I cleared my throat and swallowed. "I'm not going."

Penny looked at me and patted me on the back. "My cousin Roger said that once, too, when his family moved," she said. "He called up my mom and asked to move in."

"Did she let him?" I asked anxiously.

"Yeah," Penny said. A chill of hope shot up my spine. "But Roger missed his brothers and sisters so much that he left after two days."

"You think your mom would let me move in?" I asked.

"I'll ask her," Penny assured me.

Wil cleared her throat and adjusted her glasses. "Hey, Ro," she said to me. "I've been thinking that we might be able to help your cause."

I stopped chewing. "What do you mean?"

"I've got something better than the ghosts," she said.

She leaned closer to me and waved us all together.

"Rosie needs to be sitting on the couch in front of her parents the next time something happens," Wil said. "She needs them to be her witnesses. It's the ultimate alibi in this case."

"A what?" Molly asked.

"An alibi is when you have something or someone to prove that you weren't at the scene of the crime," Wil explained. "All our work has to be done when Rosie is in the house, doing her homework."

"You sure about this?" Penny asked.

"Who can sneak out of the house at nine o'clock tonight?" Wil asked.

"Piece of cake," Molly said. "With four kids in our family, nobody will ever know I'm gone."

"I need three nights of a commitment," Wil said.

"We're going to get caught," Penny said. "And Rosie is going to get into serious trouble."

"I don't care," I told her. The thought of my friends joining me in Operation I'm Not Moving had me up off my seat.

Wednesday morning I woke up to my father's yelling to my mother in the kitchen. I peeked out the window and felt the butterflies flutter in my stomach. White toilet paper draped across our bushes and tiny trees.

"Those kids!" he said. "I'm going to get them!"

"Who did it?" my mother asked.

"Probably that Eddie," my dad said.

My heart skipped a beat. Eddie, who did have a

strong reputation as a bully, was always getting framed for something.

"Are you sure it's Eddie?" my mother asked. "Why would he do this?"

I held my breath and recalled an earlier conversation when Wil told me to "hide the motive." I hadn't understood. She said, "If they stop and think about it, they're going to know that we're behind this. So we have to be kind and sweet all the time."

The doorbell rang. I heard Wil's voice. "Good morning," Wil said to my parents. "I saw the toilet paper on your porch and wanted to see if everything is all right."

Wil's plan didn't stop there. On Thursday morning I woke up to my mother screaming. "Ew! Ew!" she squealed. "Look at all these crickets!"

I ran out of my bedroom door and my eyes almost dropped at the thick layer of jumping black crickets covering my front porch. My mother and father started jumping all over them. I slipped on a pair of cleats and joined in the craziness. Cars zoomed past and then slowed down. Passers-by gazed out their windows squinting to see the bugs. They drove away with their mouths in big O's.

Operation I'm Not Moving was proceeding as planned. By the end of the week everybody on Broadway knew about the bugs, the toilet paper, and the ghosts. Our house was totally creepy and disgusting. I couldn't be happier.

My father remained in a lousy mood on Friday night and Saturday morning. He kept asking me if I knew who was behind the bugs, but I tried to convince him otherwise. "Maybe it's some special kind of bug season," I said.

He shook his head. My mother ordered me to pick up my belongings, dust and vacuum my bedroom. I sat down on the couch.

"Now!" my father's voice boomed.

I did as I was ordered and returned to my spot on the couch. I went to turn on the television and my father said, "No TV."

I clicked my tongue and stared outside at the rain.

"Do you want me to go out and play in the rain?" I asked. "Most people wouldn't even let their dogs out in this kind of weather."

"Watch it," he warned.

"Sorry," I quipped.

"We need to keep things quiet during the open house," he explained. "Read a book."

I wanted to scream. This was so unfair. I was a prisoner in a home that soon would not be my own.

"Maybe you could go over to Sleepy's," my father suggested.

"He's not home," I said.

Even if my best friend was, I couldn't give my father the satisfaction of removing me from the premises. One by one, the couples and realtors walked through the doors. I gave them each a mean, spiteful look. When my mother's steely eyes got ahold of me, I put my nose back in my book. After fifteen minutes of listening to Frank, the annoying salesman, rave about my house, I jumped up from the couch, ran down into my basement, and hid under the stairs. I wanted to jump and scare the life out of the next person who was serious enough to come downstairs and look at the guts of our house. When nobody came, I breathed a huge sigh of relief. The phone rang and I bolted from my hiding spot.

"Hello," I said.

"Ro?" Wil asked.

"Yeah?"

"How'd it go?"

"Nobody looked too serious," I said.

"Yes!" she cheered. "I'd better get off the phone just in case the line is tapped."

"You're crazy," gasped Molly, who was on another extension.

"I'd rather be safe than sorry," Wil whispered. "See you at the game tomorrow. Tell Rico to wear his best sweat suit and be ready to coach."

"'Cause we're going to win," Molly added.

Rico left me alone with my mother and father once again that night while he ran around town with Natalie. After chipping away at some homework, I eventually fell asleep on my bedroom floor with piles of baseball cards around me. In the morning Rico came into my room and laughed.

"I don't know why you even have a bed in here," he said. "You love that floor."

I pushed myself up off the hard carpet.

"Wil said to wear your best sweat suit," I told him.

He grinned. "I can't wait!" he said. "Johnny and Felipe are coming to officiate."

"Oh, no," I said. "Not them."

"What?" he asked. "They're my friends."

"They're always goofing off," I said. "This is serious. They'd better not laugh at us thinking it's some kind of joke."

"You worry too much," he said. "You need to take a load off your mind and just enjoy being a kid."

Frustration ran through me. "You're not afraid of moving?"

He shrugged. My heart dropped. I needed him on my side.

"What are you going to do?" I asked. "Stay or go?"

"I might stay and get my own place here," he said.

"Can I stay with you?" I asked in excitement. I saw all my dreams coming true. I'd have my own little room. I'd help out with the cooking and grocery shopping. Maybe I could even have my own separate phone line. "Please, Rico. Please!" I begged. "I promise I'll do the dishes, clean my room, sleep in my bed. I'll even pitch in on the rent. I can pick up a job doing something. Maybe delivering papers, shoveling snow . . ."

"Time out," he said. "We don't even know if we're going for sure."

"What do you mean?" I asked.

"It still might not happen."

Butterflies fluttered in my stomach.

"For now," he said, "let's worry about winning this football game today."

Rico and I went down to the park an hour early. I lined up all the equipment neatly and started organizing our bench area. Wil came jogging across the park dragging her helmet and shoulder pads. "Ro!" she called out. "You're going to be hitting some serious holes today! I'm clearing the whole field for you."

I laughed as she tripped over her shoelaces.

"Hey, Ric," Wil said. "Are your boys coming today?"

My brother nodded. "I told them you're paying them big bucks to ref."

"That's right!" she said. "The check will be in the mail."

Wil looked at me and winked. My eyes wandered over in the distance and stopped on Molly and her little sister, Annie. Annie looked like she was going to fall over as she walked with Molly's fat helmet loose on her head. Penny, Angel, Anita, and Mary turned the corner and joined the pack.

Phoebe's Bombers pulled up in a van next to the field and jumped out.

"They're going down," Molly said. "And it isn't going to be pretty."

Dozens of people started making their way onto the sidelines. Felipe and Johnny showed up in black-and-white striped shirts. They joked around with some of the players and with Rico. Wil quickly hushed any giggling girls and set the two refs straight.

"We want people to see us as serious," Wil said.

"Sorry," Felipe said. "We're just trying to have some fun."

"We *will* have fun," she said. "Once we prove to all those who don't believe that we can play, too."

Felipe and Johnny looked at each other and shrugged. Rico retreated to his spot on the sidelines and watched the Bombers sprint through their warm-ups. I looked over at their tallest player, who happened to be looking right back at me.

"What's up, Shorty?" she said.

I looked over my right shoulder and then my left.

"Yeah, you," she said. "The little one."

I stared at her dull blue eyes, tiny round mouth, and chiseled face. I snapped a picture of her in my head and walked away.

"Bring it in, Ballplayers!" my brother called out.

As we ran to the sidelines, we slapped each other's helmets and cheered. I looked up and saw my dad sipping a cup of coffee as he stood on the sidelines. He winked at me. I tried to smile but only half my face lifted before I looked away.

"Let's go, Blue!" Sweet P. said. "Huddle up!"

We all huddled together with our bulky equipment and waited for Penny's command. "All right, Blue," she said. "What are we made of?"

"Heart and guts!" we all screamed.

The growing crowd erupted in cheers. I looked up and spotted my mother. She sat nervously with one arm across her chest and the other holding her chin. She shut her eyes tightly. She was praying—praying that I didn't get hurt.

My brother's friends Felipe and Johnny had tried kidding around with me during warm-ups, but Wil hushed them up quickly. As game time grew closer, their smiles disappeared.

"These girls are ready to play," Felipe said to my brother.

"I told you," my brother said.

"Go, Ballplayers!" Mrs. O'Malley yelled.

Mr. Harris and Mr. O. clapped loudly as we stormed onto the field and lined up for the kickoff. The Bombers took their positions. Jen got a running start and booted the ball down to their end. The player directly across from me received the pass. Now it was up to me to dodge the maze of traffic and track her down. I sprinted forward like I was on fire and then waited for the runner to make a move. She broke right. I stutter-stepped, spun, and broke through one blocker. The runner went left, and then Wil made her change her mind.

"Ahhh!" Wil screamed.

Thump. My body felt like it was cracking as I wrapped it around my opponent. Penny and Molly dived on top of me to make it a double-decker sandwich.

"Yeah! Yeah!" Penny cheered.

I jumped up and was on my feet before I gave the pain a chance to hit. On the next series of plays, our defense smothered the quarterback. The Bombers couldn't move the ball in three downs, so they were forced to punt.

"Rosie," Mr. O. said. "You take the return."

I ran back into the backfield and waited as the ball hung in the air. It stung as it fell into my hands. I lost my breath for a second and then took off like a cannon. I saw an opening and went for it. But then a huge body appeared out of nowhere. I tried putting on the brakes, but it was too late. I hit a brick body and slid down to the ground.

"Rosa!" my mother screamed.

"Atta way, Shorty," a girl stood over me and sneered.

Molly and Wil each grabbed me by the armpits and

pulled me up. When my mom took two steps on the field, I returned to the real world.

"I'm fine," I snapped. She took a deep breath and returned to her spot on the sideline.

"Stay on your feet!" my dad yelled. "Stay tough!"

As usual, he was never happy with anything I did. I flicked a switch in my mind and shut my father out.

For the entire first half, both teams struggled offensively. But it was clear by the way we threw our bodies against the ground that the girls weren't just trying to prove a point or have fun.

"Blood and guts!" Mr. Harris cheered. "Show 'em, Ballplayers! Show 'em!"

We settled down in the second half and cut down on our turnovers. With Sweet P. comfortable in the driver's seat, our team ran circles around the Bombers. Wil, Anita, Mary, and Jen didn't let anybody touch Penny as she sat back and lofted perfect passes to open hands. On one play we ran a screen pass. I grabbed the leather in my hands and snuck right down the center of the field. I juked right and left. Then I spun out of the last tackler's grasp and crossed the end zone. The crowd roared. I turned and chest-butted all my teammates. We laughed and cheered as our plastic shoulder pads smacked together. Then I stopped in front of the one girl I had taken a picture of in my mind—the player who called me the "little one." I looked straight up into her sweaty face and said, "Now who's the little one?"

The Ballplayers ran away with the first victory in the League with a score of 20–6. After the game the boys came up to us.

"I didn't even know you were here," Wil said. "There were so many people we didn't see you."

J. J. shook his head. "I was just going to come over and say 'nice game' and be a good guy, and this is the kind of thanks I get?"

Pete the Creep pulled up on his rusty bicycle. "Who won?" he asked.

"We did," Molly said.

"The other team must have been really bad," Pete said with a chuckle.

Pete had made his stupid cracks and comments before, but this was totally out of line. He didn't even come to the game.

"Take your sorry bike and go home," Molly said.

"Nobody cares what you think," I added.

He raised his eyebrows and gave me an evil smile. He looked over to Sleepy, who was talking privately with Rico.

"Hey, Sleep," Pete said.

My best friend's sad eyes looked over to us.

"Tell your girlfriend to keep her mouth shut," he said.

My brother stood up straight and watched as Pete rode away. I wanted Rico and Sleepy to chase him down the street just to scare the life out of him. They didn't move. I thought about picking up something and beaming Pete on the back of his head. I turned back to Rico and Sleepy. They went back to their serious conversation as if Pete's comments had been a minor distraction. They didn't care about what he said. Whatever they were talking about seemed far more important. A chill of fear shot up my spine.

Something had to be wrong.

Chapter Eleven

Just as Wil promised, Operation I'm Not Moving continued later that same night. At precisely 18:35, military time, I heard the tap on my window. My heart skipped a beat. I raced across the room, eagerly anticipating Phase III. I held my breath as I quietly slid open my window. Dozens of fake animals and statues grazed on my front lawn. I saw bodies move in the dark and heard Molly burst into a giggle.

"Shhh!" Wil said.

Penny and Angel lugged a big, fat ceramic pig and dropped it right next to our For Sale sign. Then they sprinted away and hid in the bushes.

"Polly the Pig will be quite an attraction," Wil whispered loudly.

I grabbed my rope, jumped out my window, and stuck the landing.

"What are you doing?" Wil whispered loudly.

I ran over to the side of my house.

"I can't let you do this without me," I said.

"Get your butt back inside now!" Wil said.

"No," I shot back.

"If he sees you out here," Penny said, "he'll think you've done it all."

"I don't care."

"Why are we doing this again?" Molly asked. "It seems kind of stupid now that I think about it."

"We're just trying to show a little neighborly love to Mr. Jones," Wil said proudly. "A big 'Please don't leave' card is being passed around the neighborhood as we speak."

"You're still moving, aren't you, Ro?" Penny asked.

"They're moving," I insisted. "Not me."

The latch of my back gate scraped open, and we all shrieked. In a heartbeat we tore across my lawn as we sprinted to our hiding spots. Then my father's deep voice called out, "Girls! I know it's you. Come out right now!"

I eyed my bedroom window and thought of all the different angles I could take to avoid my father and climb back inside. Then his voice boomed, "Rosalinda!" and I surrendered before he had a chance to embarrass me with his temper. One by one we gathered in the dark and stood silent and scared.

"Every single one of you in the house," my father ordered.

"Why?" I whined. "They didn't do anything!"

I could feel my father's anger in the dark of night. He paused and then the streetlight caught his intense eyes.

"I'm calling all their parents so they know what kind of pranks they've been pulling."

All my friends held their breath. My neck tightened.

"No!" I snapped. "It's not their fault! They didn't do anything."

"Umm, excuse me for a sec," Wil said. "But I think I'd like to add something."

Her soft, shaky voice calmed the air. "For the record, We didn't do anything criminal."

"You stole other people's property," my father pointed out.

"We borrowed it," I explained. "We're going to return it."

"Do you think this is funny?" my father's voice boomed.

Wil started to stutter. "It . . . It . . . It was just our way of show . . . . showing . . . our affection for you and your family."

"The crickets? The toilet paper?" he gasped. "You call that affectionate?"

"She doesn't know what she's talking about," Penny said, jumping in for the save. "I'm sorry, Mr. J., for causing a mess. It was stupid. We shouldn't have—"

"No, it wasn't stupid," I said. "I wanted you to do it!"

My father reprimanded my friends and said that their parents would be notified. But it was late, and he let them go as long as they promised to return all the animals to their proper owners. Wil wrapped her arms around Polly the Pig's head and Angel hoisted Polly's butt off the ground. I put my hand over my mouth so my father wouldn't hear me giggle.

"In the house—now!" he said to me.

I walked straight for my window.

"What are you doing?" he asked.

"Going back in my window," I said.

"Use the front door," he ordered.

"No," I said curtly. "I don't want to."

He huffed and said, "I don't want you to ruin the window frame."

"Who cares?" I asked. "It's not going to be our house anymore."

"That's it!" he screamed. I looked around and saw some lights flick on and heads peek out windows. "No more football for you."

"Then I'll run away," I said.

We bickered back and forth until my mother ran outside on the lawn and rushed us into the house. "The whole neighborhood is listening to you two mules," she said. "Have a little respect for our family."

We all went to sleep mad at each other. After a few days the tension faded just enough for me to reverse my father's decision barring me from football practice. Rico picked me up at five P.M. Thursday night. We loaded all the equipment in his trunk and drove down to the park together. Rico talked the whole way about how much he was working out and how his agent thought he had a shot with another team for more money and playing time. I wanted to be thrilled, but I couldn't even force myself to act excited. Rico had his life outside of Broadway Ave. He would leave again soon for months to play ball. And I would be in a foreign place with complete strangers.

"Have a little faith, kid," he said.

"Can't you just get an apartment so we can live on Broadway still?" I asked.

"Well," he said. "Natalie and I talked about moving in together."

I needed a time-out. "What?" I asked.

"Yeah," he added. "It might be best for both of us."

Just as he parked the car and opened up the door, a person tapped on my window. I turned and it was Miss Lopez, smiling and waving. I stared at her blankly. She frowned and then pulled open my door.

"What's wrong?" she asked.

"Nothin'," I shot back.

"I thought you'd be a little more excited to see me," she said. "You've been bugging me forever to come."

I remained silent as I went to the trunk. Rico cleared his throat and said, "Hi, I'm Rosie's brother, Rico. You must be Miss Lopez."

She nodded, smiled, and shook his hand. Then she stared back at me, waiting for an explanation. I refused to speak.

"Rosie talks about you all the time," Rico added. "She reads a lot more now, too."

Miss Lopez nodded again as my brother covered for me. I threw the equipment over my shoulder and walked away.

"She's a little upset over this moving thing," Rico said quietly as I walked away. He failed to mention the part about his moving in with his lousy girlfriend. But I couldn't give up hope. Miss Lopez could still charm him with her athletic ability and cool personality. I spun around, eager to turn on a new attitude, but then stopped in my tracks as Miss Lopez marched right up to me.

"I take the time to come out here and all I get is your attitude?" she asked. My eyes grew wide in fear as my teacher blew off her steam. "You think you're the only one with problems? That it's the end of the world if you move out of here? Like there aren't far more tragic, sad things in life?"

I immediately recognized this conversation as a lecture and did not give any input. I simply stared at the ground, hiding my ashamed eyes under my cap. The Ballplayers and Rico walked past us pretending like they didn't hear Miss Lopez's tirade.

She calmed down after a few minutes, stayed for practice, and cheered on my team. I watched her out of the corner of my eye whenever she moved closer or talked to my brother. I looked for a little sparkle in his eye and waited for him to rest a soft hand on her shoulder. But they cheered with their eyes glued to the field. I had myself convinced that they were both just playing games with each other. It was up to me to show them that they were meant to be together.

At the end of practice Miss Lopez took off before I had a chance to say goodbye.

"What's wrong?" Penny asked me as I walked off the field alone.

"I was just thinking about something," I said. Then I changed my mind about telling anyone my matchmaking plans. "Forget it. Just forget it."

I didn't see Rico again until Saturday morning.

Although I was annoyed at him for having left me again, I didn't waste any time getting to what concerned me most. As we tossed the ball back and forth on the front lawn, I started my line of questioning.

"Isn't Miss Lopez so nice?" I asked.

He nodded. "But you really got under her skin."

"She gets like that sometimes with me," I said.

"I thought what she said to you was great," he added with a smile.

I didn't appreciate his comment, but I let it go.

"She's really pretty, too," I said. Then I paused and looked at my brother. "Don't you think?"

"She is," he said.

My heart skipped a beat.

"She really likes baseball," I added.

"She told me," he said.

"She did? What else did you talk about?"

"You," he said.

My shoulder dropped and I sighed. "Anything besides me?"

Rico's eyes stared up in the distance and he grinned. "Hey, man!" he called out. "What's up, Sleep?"

The frustration grew inside of me. "What else did you and Miss Lopez talk about?" I said firmly. My brother took the ball out from under his arm and threw a line drive to my best friend. Sleepy's sad eyes looked the ball right into his glove.

"Go get your bat, kid," my brother said.

I trudged into the house and picked up my bat. On the way back outside, Rico had his hand resting on Sleepy's shoulder and then rubbed his back. Sleepy stared at the ground as if he was going to cry. I sprinted up to both of them.

"What's wrong?" I said in fear.

"Nothin'," Sleepy said. "Let's play some ball."

I looked at my brother, begging for an explanation. He cocked his arm back, winked, and said, "Catch this one, Shorty."

I glared at Rico and he grinned.

Helen Hart's Tigers were supposed to stink. Wil gave us the scouting report and said Helen had a "wet noodle of an arm."

"She can't throw, and nobody on their team can run," Wil assured us.

To our surprise, the Tigers ran and threw like all-pros. Most of the girls we didn't recognize, which made Wil suspicious.

"They must have flown girls in from other states to beat us," Wil said. "I'm going to have to investigate."

"Yeah," Molly agreed. "They must have cheated."

Guilty or innocent of violating unwritten League rules, we lost 14–7.

"Let it go," Penny said. "We can still get them back in the playoffs."

The only highlight of the game was seeing my brother and Miss Lopez huddling together. I imagined that my cool, suave brother would find a way to ask her out on a romantic date. She'd pretend like she was busy, but then she'd accept, knowing that a date with my sweet brother was something she couldn't refuse.

After the game I saw my brother and Miss Lopez talking again and my nerves tingled. A bunch of the parents mingled on the sidelines as we gathered our smelly equipment.

"These things stink so bad," Angel said as she pinched her nose. "You all sweat too much."

"It's leftover funk from the boys," Penny said.

"Yeah," Wil added. "Girls' sweat is supposed to smell like flowers."

"Yours doesn't," Molly quipped.

We laughed for the first time that afternoon. I walked up to my parents and overheard the end of the conversation my father was having with Molly's and Penny's parents.

"Thanks for your support," my father said. "I know you mean well. But it looks like everything is a go. It's just a great opportunity for me and my family."

Penny's idea of getting the parents to lay the guilt trip on my mother and father seemed to be failing miserably. I should have warned my friends about my dad. The more that people doubted him, the more he wanted to prove them wrong.

"It doesn't sound good," Wil whispered to me.

I smiled, pretending not to hear any of it. I watched Miss Lopez jog up to us with a big smile on her face. My heart filled with hope. Rico must have asked her out. She waved and then zoomed right past us.

"Where are you going?" I screamed.

"For a run!" she called back to me.

Then I turned to my brother as he threw the equipment bag over his arm. "We're going to bounce back next weekend," he told my friends.

"Where are you going?" I asked firmly.

"Out with Natalie," he said.

"Why?"

"What do you mean 'why'?" he shot back.

I said nothing. I marched over to my mother and stood by her. I stared at my dad, hinting strongly that I just wanted to leave.

With Operation I'm Not Moving out the window, I now needed a miracle.

Chapter Twelve

I tried to breeze right past Mr. Gordon in school on Monday, but he called out my name. I relaxed and took a deep breath, assuring myself that he had nothing on me. I had completed all my homework to keep myself eligible to play football. I hadn't blasted Pete the Creep even though I seriously considered borrowing his bike without his permission for an extended period of time. All in all, I had kept my nose clean.

"How's English class?" he asked.

"Fine," I said with a big smile.

"Quarterly reports are coming out soon," he told me. "I'm going to be meeting with Miss Lopez."

"I've done everything," I pleaded.

"It's important you get yourself on track now. next year only gets harder."

When the words *next year* came out of his mouth, I crawled into my private shell and did not say another word. *Don't even waste your time on me, Mr. G. It's hopeless. I'm leaving this school. My life is over.* But I couldn't quit. I couldn't give up after fighting the good fight, not after all the help from the Ballplayers. I thought of living in Sleepy's basement. Nobody would know I was there.

The last bell rang that afternoon, and Miss Lopez asked me to stay after class. I moped up to the front of the room and sat down in a chair. I didn't even feel like arguing. I just wanted to go home to my room and draw up a plot for what I would do if the moving trucks tried to pull in my driveway and change my life forever.

"I can see you're having a hard time," Miss Lopez said.

I just sat there staring down at the blank desktop.

"It probably would help if you talked about things, instead of holding them all in," she suggested.

"No whining" was a rule for players in our football league.

"Packing all your worries and fears inside of you isn't good," she said. "You can't carry this all by yourself."

She paused and then leaned closer to me. "Are you listening to me?"

I shrugged. She threw her hands up in the air, turned, and walked back to her desk.

"Do you have a boyfriend?" I asked.

She whipped around and raised her eyebrow. "What does this have to do with anything?"

"I was just wondering," I said.

She didn't answer.

"Do you?" I insisted.

"No," she said. "Not right now. I just broke up with a guy I had been dating for a while."

All my frustration and worry seemed to escape me for that brief moment. I had to make the most of this. "My brother wants to ask you out."

She smiled at me and shook her head. "That's funny," she said.

"Why?" I asked.

"He was telling me about his girlfriend at your game."

My eyes grew wide and I froze, trying to think of something fast. At the same time I was furious at my brother for saying anything about Natalie. "They broke up," I said. "So maybe now you can spend some time with him."

She tilted her head and rested her hand on her hip. She had a knack for picking up on large stretches of the truth from her students. "I don't think so," she said as she pulled her hair back into an elastic.

I had to draw up another strategy in my mind before I missed the bus.

"Did you hear about open dodgeball after school?" Miss Lopez asked me.

"No," I said. My heart jumped. I didn't know it was an open dodgeball day. I loved dodgeball. "Are you sure?"

She nodded. "Go down to the gym right now," she said as she looked up at the clock.

I raced out of the room and yelled goodbye. No, I wouldn't talk, but I would play dodgeball. I sprinted down the hallway, fearing that I'd be late and wondering how I could not have heard about this sooner. I turned the corner and whipped open the gym door.

"Where have you been, Ro?" Penny called out.

I jogged over to my friends. "I didn't know about it."

"I told you at lunch," Molly said. "Don't you remember?"

I shook my head.

"You all right, Ro?" Wil asked.

"Yeah," I said. "Let's play."

Our gym teacher set us up for thirty minutes of dodgeball heaven. With Anita on my right and Wil on my left, I eyed Pete as he warmed up his throwing arm across from me.

"Do know what a midget you look like standing between those two giants?" he called out.

Before anyone could reply, a ball came from out of nowhere and drilled Pete in the stomach just as he cocked his head back in laughter.

"Ugh," he moaned and then winced. He picked his head up to find his assailant.

Molly grinned and skipped up to us. "That's your wake-up call, Pete!" she yelled. "But your nightmares are just beginning!"

Adrenaline and sheer joy rushed through me. Anita, Wil, and I grinned as we gave Molly a high five.

"You wait!" Pete screamed. "Just wait! It's game time. It's over for all of you wannabe-boys."

His words stung and the whistle shrieked. It was time for Pete the Sneak to pay.

With my hands tightly gripping the ball, I felt like a heat-seeking missile. *Bam!* I nailed Dawn Miller, another notorious bully, in the knee. I had wanted to go for Pete right away, but I needed to be sneakier than the creep himself. I waited patiently to make my move.

Defensively nobody could touch me. I danced around, dodging balls and scooping up bad throws. Then I set my radar on Pete, who stayed on the right side of the floor. I ran cross-court, acting as if I were going to throw left and then spun at the last minute and focused on Pete's long, skinny nose. His eyes grew wide and he slowly raised his hands. I grunted as I let the ball go, held my follow through, and waited for the result. The ball slammed Pete in the chin. His face jerked left. He cupped his chin and then screamed to our gym teacher, "Rosie hit me in the face!"

Our gym teacher waved him off, and he screamed again. "She did!" he said. "It shouldn't count!"

When the teacher waved the whiner back into the game, Molly and Wil launched their protest. "I vote to change that rule," Wil said. "Can we take a vote?"

"No," the teacher replied.

"There's no whining where we come from!" Wil pleaded.

While the teacher refused to budge, Pete grinned like a devil. He looked over and stuck out his tongue at Molly and Wil as the teacher turned away. At the same time a ball lofted high in the air and then fell straight down on his chest. I turned to see who had been responsible. Anita stood tall and yelled, "Have a seat, Pete!"

The glory washed over the shortest and tallest ballplayers in the building. I ran up to Anita and jumped high in the air to reach her extended hands. We slapped each other with a hard, stinging, yet so rewarding double high five. Then Pete turned into a person we didn't recognize, far worse than we'd ever seen.

"You're all so fat and ugly," he said. "That's why you're so good at football."

"Why don't you be a big person for once and act like a human being?" Wil said.

"As big and fat as you?" he snapped back.

The whistle shrieked and shrieked and shrieked. Our gym teacher released her lips from the black whistle, sucked in one deep breath, and then screamed, "That's enough!" Then she kicked us all out of the gym.

"I'm sorry! We're sorry!" Wil pleaded to the teacher. "We should have listened to you."

"It's too late," the teacher said.

"Could you have warned us?" Molly asked.

"You all know better," she said. "You keep treating each other like that and you don't deserve to have any fun."

"One more try?" Wil begged.

"Get out and stay out!" the teacher yelled.

We all hustled out of the gym, propelled by the anger in our teacher's voice. When we reached the hallway, Penny finally spoke. "I can't believe we've been streeted," she said in disbelief.

The Ballplayers and I started walking home. Then I spotted Rico's car in the distance, heading straight for us. He pulled up and rolled down the window.

"Need a ride?" he asked.

"What's your fare?" Penny said.

"You can't afford it," my brother replied with a grin.

"All I ask is that you stay away from my house."

"Sorry about that," Penny added nervously. I laughed knowing how funny Rico thought it was that my friends had participated in Operation I'm Not Moving.

"I forgive you," Rico said.

We all jumped in the car with giggles and recapped how much fun it was to pull all the pranks on my parents. "You know we were just playing around," Molly said. "We just don't want you to leave."

"I'll see if we can offer you a paid coaching position," Wil said. "What do you think?"

Rico tipped his head back and smiled in amusement. "I'll have to contact my agent first," he joked.

We dropped off all the Ballplayers at their houses. I bragged to Rico about how Anita and I had given Pete the Sneak his due that day. He smiled while I told the story, as if he had been right there with me.

"Where's Sleepy?" Rico asked.

"He was sick from school today," I said.

"Maybe you should call him," he suggested.

"I will," I said.

We pushed open the front door, and my mother greeted us with a warm smile. I hadn't seen her bright teeth and happy brown eyes in so long.

"I have some good news," she said.

"I don't even want to know what our new house looks like," I moaned. "So don't even tell me."

"No!" she blurted out as she shook her head. She stopped to catch her breath.

"What is it, Ma?" Rico asked.

"We might not be moving after all!" my mother shouted.

I dropped my school bag and froze. "Really?" I gasped.

She nodded and said, "The deal might not go through."

Rico stood straight-faced. I tugged on his sleeve and smiled up at him, wanting for my brother to celebrate with us. He threw his keys down on the desk. "This is such a joke," he said. "I don't know what to believe anymore. It changes every minute."

"We can't give up hope," my mother assured us.

Chapter Thirteen

When Sleepy didn't show up for school the next day, I called his house the minute I walked in the door.

"Hello?" he groaned.

"Hi, it's me," I said. "What's wrong?"

"I'm sick," he replied.

"You want me to come over?"

"No," he said. "My little sister is sick, too."

"When are you coming back to school?" I asked.

"I don't know," he said. "Not tomorrow."

"We might not be moving," I told him, hoping to lift his spirits.

"Oh," he said. "That's good."

Then there was a long pause. Sleepy usually didn't get so run-down and he hardly ever sounded so low.

"Maybe we can play some ball over the weekend," I

assured him. "That will make you feel better."

"Yeah," he said. "I guess."

When I hung up the phone, my mom came through the door. I sat on the couch wondering what was going on with my best friend.

"What's wrong?" my mother asked.

"Sleepy's sick," I said.

"He'll get better," she replied.

"Did you hear anything about Dad's job?"

She shook her head. "He's been out late every night in meetings. I don't know what's going on. It changes every minute."

I wished his bosses would get their acts together and just make a lousy decision instead of playing this game of cat and mouse. They had no idea that they were toying with my life, my future plans to be a star on Broadway Ave.

"You must have football practice tonight," my mother said.

I nodded. She went to the cupboard and eyed the shelves.

"All I do is say my prayers that you don't break any bones out there," she said. "I can't handle any more stress right now."

"I won't break anything, Ma," I pleaded as I opened up a textbook.

"You'd better run your tail off every time you get your hands on that ball," she said.

"Didn't you see me last week?" I asked.

She nodded. "But you let them get too close."

I huffed in frustration, shook my head, and started my

homework. An hour later I finished all my work, devoured some spaghetti, and loaded up Rico's car with football equipment.

At practice Wil handed out a stapled packet of paper. "What's this?" I asked.

"The scouting report," she said.

We all raised our eyebrows and flipped through the pages of diagrams and lists of the strengths and weaknesses of every player on Tasha's Trashers.

"Did you do all of this?" Molly asked.

"No, not all of it," Wil said. "I had some help."

"Who?" Rico asked.

"A secret spy," she said.

"Hold up," Penny called out. "You stole all their plays?"

"No!" Wil shot back defensively. "If they're dumb enough to leave their playbooks behind on public property, then we have legally every right to taking a look."

"Did you find it?" Penny asked.

Wil did not respond.

"Who found it?" Angel asked.

"I can't tell you," Wil asked. "If Tasha's team finds out, this guy is a goner."

Instead of lecturing Wil or any of us on sports ethics and conduct, Rico flipped page by page through the playbook and shrugged. "This is how they do it in the big leagues," he explained.

"We are in the big leagues," Wil insisted. She then reached into her backpack and pulled out a second pile of papers.

"What are those?" Rico asked.

"I watched the videotape of our first two games and jotted down some of my observations," she said. "We're sagging too much on defense, and the O-line is not making clean, forceful blocks. We're sloppy, really sloppy."

I looked at Wil in disbelief with all my friends. She always did twice as much homework as everyone else. I couldn't imagine how she found time to put all of this together. I was the one with the idea, yet Wil did all the work.

"Do you want me to do anything?" I asked, feeling guilty.

"Yeah," she said. "All of us need to spread the word that we're having a round-robin tournament this weekend."

"What's that?" Anita asked.

"All the teams are going to be there," she said. "We're all playing each other in short games and then going on to the next team."

"Oh, great," Jen said.

"What do you mean, 'oh, great?'" Wil asked defensively. "We just need to be prepared to play everyone. Rico will make sure we're ready. Right, Ric?"

All eyes turned to my brother and he nodded. "Maybe we should start by taking the field sometime tonight. Is everyone here?"

We all looked around and noticed we were two short of a full team.

"We're missing Precious and Mookey," Penny said.

"Oh, great," Molly scoffed. "What are we going to do without our water girls?"

"Mo, that's enough," Penny said.

"Come on, P.," she said, "They didn't even show up for one of the games and they're always late."

"They don't want to mess up their hair," Anita added.

Just at that moment Precious and Mookey jumped out of a car and ran toward us. They giggled at first. But when they looked up and saw our scowling faces as we strapped on our helmets, whatever they found to be funny was not anymore. They ran over to us, eyes staring at the ground. Our silent treatment made them out of breath and jittery.

"Everybody huddle up!" Wil announced.

Nobody moved.

"Let's go, ladies!" Wil called out. "I said huddle up!"

Everyone dragged their equipment toward Wil and threw their hands in. "We've got a big weekend coming up. Probably the biggest weekend in our sports careers to date."

Penny and I looked at each other and we smiled at Wil's transformation into a totally nuts NFL head coach.

"If we don't go out and mix it up in practice, we're never going to be ready for Sunday," she said. "It's going to be a dogfight out there. I mean a dogfight! We need to get down and dirty. Throw some bodies. Be mean. Be animals. You got that? Do you hear me?"

We all nodded. Wil clicked her tongue. Mookey dropped her bow and bent over to pick it up.

"Precious and Mookey," Wil called out. They bit their lips and looked nervous. "Get rid of those bows, forget the giggling, and show us some heart and guts today!"

Precious and Mookey quickly removed all of their bows and nodded their heads for about five seconds.

Then they raised their helmets and stuffed them on their plain heads.

"On three," Penny called out. "One, two three . . ."

"Heart and guts!" we all screamed.

As we stormed onto the field, Rico and the other coaches clapped their hands together and called out the drills. Wil herself practiced what she preached and ran through the drills as if she had a fire under her. The pace quickened and our timing clicked in synch. We played some serious football until it was so dark we couldn't see the ball. Parents waited in the parking lot, impatiently pacing outside their cars. My mother even drove up, wondering what was taking so long. Nobody was mad at Rico for keeping us because we wanted to stay. Even Precious and Mookey. When the last whistle blew, we gathered under the closest light. Streaks of dirt and sweat covered our cheerleaders' faces. They bent down on one knee and gasped for air.

My brother listened to us suck in as much oxygen as possible. Then a huge grin spread across his face. "Now, that's the way to play ball!" Rico roared.

"Way to go Ballplayers!" Mr. Harris cheered.

We all exploded into cheers and jumped up for our last "team" cheer. Before we took three steps, Wil added an announcement.

"We're having a pasta party on Saturday night," Wil said proudly.

"Whose house?" Penny asked.

Wil winced and then looked around our huddle. "Any volunteers? It's bring your own pasta. We'll just all cook it together and clean up the mess."

After her dad nodded his approval, Molly called out, "Be at my house at eight."

We all limped off the field dragging our burning muscles and equipment along. I went home that night, showered, and fell asleep with my homework in my bed.

I saw very little of my father for the next few days. My mother kept telling me that he was wrapped up in meetings, and I didn't ask what the meetings were about. Grilling my mother about things she didn't know would only drive the both of us crazy.

Sleepy came over on Saturday afternoon, and we ran through our once-a-month mini-Olympics of baseball, soccer, and basketball. In between events I complained to him about the moving situation, and he just told me not to worry.

"What?" I asked. "How can you say that?"

"You don't even know if you're going," he pointed out.

"Well, what if we do?" I asked.

"You don't know yet," he replied.

"So?" I said. "Don't I have the right to worry?"

He just shook his head. We played for another half-hour or so, but something just wasn't the same. Sleepy jogged lazily through most of our games, and we didn't thrive on beating each other like we normally did.

"Are you still sick?" I asked.

"I don't think so," he said. "But my mom does. I'd better get home before she does. She won't want me outside sweating so much in the cold."

We said goodbye and I ran into the house. I piled up

all my pasta and threw a couple of juice boxes into a plastic bag.

"I'm going to Molly's," I called out to my mom. "I'll be home by eleven."

"Nine," my mother replied.

"Ten-thirty," I said.

"Ten," she called out.

"But—" I blurted.

"You'd better get out that door before I change my mind," she said.

Rico pulled up just as I hit the driveway, and I talked him into a free ride down the street. Rico parked his smooth car in Molly's driveway.

"Are you coming in?" I asked.

"I am the coach, right?" he replied.

I grinned. My brother was the coolest guy in town, taking time out on a Saturday night to be with his little sister and her team. We walked up to the house and rang the bell. All the lights were off inside. Then the door creaked open. Molly greeted us with a huge smile. I looked around into the dark living room and asked, "Where is . . ."

"Surprise!" The whole house shook. The lights flicked on. Balloons and signs covered the walls.

"What?" I asked. "Who's the party for?"

"You!" Wil called out. "It's your going-away party!"

My heart sank. I didn't smile. I couldn't celebrate. I simply froze in disbelief as if this were some nightmare. Rico rested his hand on my shoulders and gently directed me into the room. We smiled and high-fived all my teammates as I stumbled through the living room in front of him. Penny's eyes got ahold of mine. "Are you going to be all right?" she whispered.

Tears and I never mixed in front of my friends, but that moment broke my heart. Just when I thought I'd completely lose it, Wil started cracking jokes and I faked some good laughs. My lungs felt tight as I took slow, painful breaths. But each one got easier as my friends kept me laughing. Rico waited about an hour, until I seemed steady on my own. The girls all cheered for him as he left.

"Be good tonight!" Wil said. "No trouble! We've got an afternoon of football waiting for us tomorrow."

Right after dinner the phone rang. Molly rushed to it, said hello, and then screamed for Wil. She came running with a big grin.

"Who is it?" Wil asked her.

"I don't know," Molly said. "Some guy."

Our whole team burst into a bunch of excited OOOOHHHHs. Wil smiled like a champion, loving all the attention.

"It's some adult guy," Molly said to clarify.

We all groaned in disappointment.

"Who could it be?" Wil asked.

We all listened quietly and giggled as Wil took the phone. As we waited, I looked up at Precious and Mookey and smiled. They weren't wearing any bows or pink outfits. Molly even offered them a drink.

Wil kept saying "uh-huh, uh-huh," and acting all serious on the phone.

Molly punched her on the arm. "Who is it?" she whispered impatiently.

"Looking forward to seeing you tomorrow, sir," Wil said, and then she slowly and deliberately hung up the phone. She turned to us and screamed, "Ahhhh!" Then she started jumping up and down.

"Tell us!" Molly screamed. "Tell us now!"

Wil danced around and caught her breath. "It's the newspaper," she said. "They're writing a story on the League!"

"Tomorrow?" Penny gasped.

"Yes!" she said. "This is huge!"

We all started cheering and high-fiving one another.

"Soon the whole country will be all over this story," Wil stated boldly as she looked up at one of the walls. She waved her hand in the air as if she were reading a sign. "Ballplayers start first girls' football league!" she announced. "I love it, I love it, I love it!"

The hoots and hollers followed. My nerves tingled with excitement.

"This is just the beginning," Penny said. "Next year is going to be even bigger!"

My heart stopped. I slumped down in my seat and stared blankly around at all my great friends. There would be no next year for me. My life would never be the same without them.

A few minutes later Wil ordered Precious and Mookey into the kitchen. They came out with an armful of wrapped presents and walked right toward me. I sat there shaking my head.

"What's wrong?" Mookey asked.

I started to stutter. "I . . . I . . ."

"These are for you, Rosie," Precious said.

The tears formed a tidal wave in my chest. I turned to Molly. Her bright blue eyes saddened. Penny rested her arm on my shoulder. Wil and Angel tried to console me, but I didn't hear anything. I couldn't take their gifts. I couldn't listen to any more good-byes. Before I exploded into a mess of tears and emotion, I bolted toward the front door.

"I'm not moving!" I screamed as I sprinted down Broadway Avenue. My whole team followed after me. They sounded like a herd of elephants.

"Wait! Wait!" Penny begged.

I spun around and stopped on a dime. They all put on the brakes and ran into each other like dominoes.

"I'm sorry," I said. "I just want to go home."

I wiped the tears from my cheeks. I had taken so much pride in never letting my friends see me cry. *Now look at me!* I took a deep breath. "I know you're just trying to do the right thing," I said. "But if I take those gifts from you, it will mean I'm really leaving. I can't give up hope."

No one forced me back to the party. I turned to my house and they walked with me silently. We said our goodbyes, and I thanked them.

"We're playing for you, Ro," Wil said. "This season is dedicated to you."

A lump formed in my throat as I turned and walked into my house dazed and hurt from all the emotions racking my body.

"Where's your coat?" my father asked.

I looked up at him and my lip started to quiver. "What do you care?" I shot back.

His face flushed an angry red. I knew I shouldn't have said it. But he didn't know what I had just put up with for the sake of bettering his career.

"Sit down," he said firmly.

My mother emerged from the kitchen and sat down on the couch. She waved me over to sit next to her. I sat on the edge of the couch, back tight, legs stiff.

"We're in this together," my father said.

I waited for him to get to the bad news.

"I'm taking the job the week after next," he said. "We'll be moving in about three weeks. Someone is going to make an offer on the house this week."

"Who's buying our house?" I blurted out.

My father didn't name names. He knew better. I was at the end of my rope. I would have done something crazy.

"If you don't tell me," I said, "I'm not going anywhere!"

He refused to leak any information and tried to keep his composure. I scoffed, and then muttered, "You're going to have to drag me out of here."

"We will if that's the way you want it," he said.

I looked at my mother, and she rested her hand on my back and rubbed it. "It's what's best for our family," she said.

My heart sank. She couldn't be on his side. I jumped up from the couch and sprinted down the hallway. "I'm never talking to you again!"

I went into my room and buried my head in my pillow. After a few minutes of silent, painful sobs and sniffles, I came up from my hiding and looked at my calendar. I took a look at the dates and decided when would be the best day to make a break for it. My father had given me no reason to stay. I had to escape—the sooner, the better.

Chapter Fourteen

I woke up the next morning to the smell of my mother's sweet pancakes.

"Rosa!" she called out. "Time for breakfast."

I thought about fasting as a form of protest. Then my mouth started watering. I went out into the kitchen with my mind made up that I could eat, but that I would not speak. They never listened to anything I said anyway.

"Good morning," my mother said.

I sat down at the table and dug into the stack of fluffy golden brown cakes. I poured on extra syrup. As I started eating, I picked up the sports section.

"Don't read at the table," my mother said.

I kept my eyes on the page.

"Rosa!" my mother warned.

I huffed and threw the paper on the chair next to me. I finished breakfast as quickly as possible.

"Get dressed for church," my mother said.

I glared at her as I left the kitchen, mad that she was not feeling any sympathy. She just gave out orders. Just like my father.

I didn't look at him the entire morning or during the ride to church. I sat through the service with my arms crossed. On the way home my mother and father talked as if I weren't even there. They didn't care about my protest. They didn't care about anything. When my father dropped my mother off at my aunt's house, I wanted to ask why. But I stuck to my silence. My muscles grew tight as I sat in the backseat alone.

The car moved forward and I stared out the window. I started to count to ten. At eight my father began. "I cannot begin to explain to you how much it hurts me to see you go through this," he said.

Yeah, right.

"I did not sleep one minute last night," he said. "I thought about leaving all our family and friends and our life here . . ."

Then his voice cracked and tears I had never ever seen from my father came pouring out of his sad, tired eyes. I started to shake, not wanting to cry. Then a stroke of guilt thumped me in the chest and the tears would not stop. My father sniffled and sobbed. "I'm trying to do what's best for our family," he said. "I want to give you more. I want you to have a good college education, and I need money and a job that will allow me help you and your mother."

Catch Shorty by Rosie

I quickly wiped my tears with the back of my sleeve.

"Please, Rosie," he begged. "Know that this is going to hurt me, too. Leaving my family. I've lived here all my life. I love my family and friends as much as you do. I love you, Rosie. I do love you."

His words made all my pain worse. I stared down in my lap as my father and I cried together. My head spun and my heart hurt. I clasped my hands together and tried to pray. But my mind drew a blank. I didn't know what to pray for anymore.

Chapter Fifteen

Rico and I left for the game that afternoon, and my mother assured us that she and my father would be down to the park in time for kickoff.

"You don't have to come if you don't want to," I told her.

My mother looked at me with surprise. "I never said we didn't want to come," she said. "We always go to your games."

"Fine," I said. "But please don't scream so much today. There are going to be a lot of reporters down there, and it's a big day for us. I don't want them thinking about how worried my mom is about me getting hurt."

"Fine, Miss Tough Girl." She sighed. "I'll do my best."

On the ride to the park I didn't say anything to Rico

about seeing my father cry or the things he said to me that morning. No words could describe how he broke down, and how awful I felt.

Although I wanted to bring up the issue one last time, I didn't ask Rico if he might want to date Miss Lopez. And I didn't beg him to find an apartment so I could stay and live on Broadway Ave. After all that had happened this morning, all I wanted to do was play football.

We played against each team for thirty minutes with a five-minute break to rotate fields. In the opening minutes of the first game, Tasha's team pushed us around, but then Wil lit a fire under us with another one of her motivational tirades.

"Dig deep and make 'em pay out there!" she screamed.

Earlier in the day when two reporters drifted toward our sidelines, scratching down notes, Wil had called a private team meeting. Penny reviewed the League rules: "No tears, no giggling, no whining, and no acting like we're just out there to have some fun."

"We've never acted like that," Molly said.

"I know," Wil said. "But people are going to be looking for a reason to say we're not good enough or strong enough. Don't give them any excuses."

I turned to Precious and Mookey. With charcoal smeared under their intense eyes and scowls on their faces, it was clear that we were all in this together.

On our fifth possession against Tasha's team, Penny connected with me on a perfect screen pass. I caught the ball, turned, and bolted down the mouth of the defense.

"Catch Shorty!" Tasha screamed.

I felt huge shadows move in on me and held on for the thumping. I wrapped up the ball tight as I received a hit from the right, then a bashing from the left. The whistle blew and then *BAM!* Tasha nailed me with one last blow.

"Late hit!" Molly screamed. "Throw her outta here!"

My lungs shrunk into a ball. No air would enter or exit. I listened to all the noise around me as I crumpled down on the ground.

"Rosa! Rosa!" my mother screamed.

When I felt her hands on my back, my lungs and heart started working again. I rolled over and huffed in frustration. "Mom, please get off the field!"

"I'm taking you home—now!" she said.

"You always told me I could do anything I wanted," I said. "Will you please just let me play football?"

My dad came over and bent down next to me. So did Rico.

"You okay, honey?" my dad asked.

I looked at him and rolled my eyes. "If you guys would all just leave me alone, I'd be able to get back up and finish this game."

One by one, my family assisted me up on my feet. Then they left me to fend for myself. I jogged back to the huddle, and the crowd roared. From that play on, all I could hear my mother screaming was "Heart! Heart!" in between her silent prayers.

Every time a linebacker crushed me, I jumped up off the ground faster than they did. Penny, Molly, and Wil cheered like mad fools for me, and I did the same for them. All the scouting reports and preparation by Wil paid off. We beat the Trashers 14–7. But the afternoon was far from over.

In between games my father pulled me aside and started reeling off a list of things I needed to improve on.

"You're always cutting left," he said. "Go right."

My dad was back to being the same ol' dad I knew. I hung my head as all my friends moved into the next game without criticism from their parents.

"On defense, hit 'em lower," he said. "Wrap 'em up tighter."

By the way he carried on at my games one would think I was being scouted by a professional football league.

"And one more thing," he began.

"I've gotta go, Dad," I said. I sprinted away from him and took the field for game two.

Right before the game started, a guy in the crowd yelled above all the others. "Come on, *girls,* let's see if you know how to play some football."

"Just go out and have some fun," another added with a laugh.

All of us turned to the offenders.

"We haven't shown you how to play already?" Rico called out.

The guy called out some more nonsense and laughed. Rico ignored him as he tried to get us to focus on his clipboard.

"Girls can't play football," a scratchy voice called out. It was like someone running their fingernails down the blackboard. I recognized the voice before I turned around.

"I'll take care of this," Molly said as she rested her hand on Wil's shoulder. We all waited to see what trouble Molly's temper would get us all into.

"Hey, Pete!" Molly said as she tossed a ball to Penny. "If you catch this football right now, then you're right, we don't know how to play. If you don't, we'd like you to take your sorry, skinny, weak self home and start lifting weights."

Rico and the coaches tried to break up this little contest, but Molly told them to wait. She gave Penny the nod and said, "Drill 'em." Pete ran right on a diagonal, right in front of the crowd. Penny cocked her arm back and fired the perfect spiral pass like a missile. The ball slapped against Pete's hands and dropped to the ground. Pete shook his stinging hands and winced in pain.

"Go home, Pete!" somebody in the crowd called out.

Not one of us cheered. We turned back to our coaches and went back to playing football.

"Let's see some heart and guts!" Mr. Harris cheered as he jogged into our huddle.

Everybody on our team played and did something positive on the field. Even Mookey caught a pass and ran like a dog was chasing her right into the end zone. She danced around in a wild celebration until Molly and Wil tackled her and she lost her breath.

"You all right down there, Mook?" Penny called out to the bottom of the pile.

Bodies uncovered the star, and Mookey bounced back up. Camera crews from the local television stations showed up and started filming. By the end of the afternoon reporters had interviewed the players, coaches, fans, and parents. We heard that somebody went up to ask Pete the Sneak some questions, but he wouldn't talk.

"He can't handle the truth," Wil said.

"But he didn't say anything bad about us," Angel added. "And for Pete, that must have been tough."

J. J., Sleepy, and Eddie came up to us.

"We can't believe all the hype," J. J. said. "This is big time."

"We told you," Molly said.

Wil ran over to us in a panic. She ripped off her helmet. "Did anybody see Oprah or Rosie here?" she asked.

Everybody shook their heads. "What about NBC, CBS, or ABC? I heard one of the big ones was here."

"It's all rumor and hype mixed together," warned Penny.

Wil sighed as she started to remove her shoulder pads.

"It's all right, Commissioner Thomas," Angel said with a grin. "We still have the finals."

Wil grinned and we all slapped her five. Miss Lopez joined our little huddle of Lincoln School kids and congratulated us on our efforts. "I can't wait to watch the news tonight."

"Are you coming to the championship next weekend?" I asked.

She nodded. "I wouldn't miss it for the world!"

Rico walked over to us and said hello to Miss Lopez.

"Miss Lopez is coming to our game next weekend!" I told him proudly.

"That's great," he said. "We could always use a coach who knows what she's doing, and somebody who can handle all of Wil's scouting reports."

Wil grinned again as the last trickle of sweat dripped from her brow. The charcoal had run down her face, and her hair fell out of her bun. I reached up and wrapped one of my arms around her, trying to hold her up.

"Thanks, Shorty," she said, and then she gave me a wink.

My mother, father, brother, and I made it through a peaceful dinner without any arguments loud enough for the neighbors to hear. Without having finished chewing my last mouthful of food, my mother rushed us all out into the living room to watch the news. When we sat down on the couch, the doorbell rang. I ran to it, hoping it was Sleepy. I smiled in anticipation until I saw a big red bow you'd put on a wreath instead of a head. It was Natalie all dressed up in a red jacket over a red-and-white striped sweater. Fat gold jewelry hung from her earlobes and neck like she was one big Christmas ornament.

"Hi," she said with a nervous smile.

She was scared of me. We both knew it. I opened the door and let her in without saying hello.

"You could have said hi," my brother said to me.

"I thought it was Sleepy," I replied.

A second of awkward silence passed. My mother and father both glared at me. Any other time they would have ordered me to my room for being rude. But it had been a while since our family had something that brought us all together, so I told them all to hurry up and sit down as I bolted toward the television. We all watched the TV, eagerly awaiting the coverage of our football league.

"Here it is!" my mother called out.

"Shhhh," I said.

The anchor told the story of our league with enthusiasm in her voice.

"What are these girls made of?" she asked. Then the camera flashed to our huddle as we screamed: "Heart and guts!"

Then the cameras cut to Penny throwing the ball and Molly catching it. On the next piece I ran the football down the middle of the field and took a hard hit but bounced back up. Butterflies fluttered in my stomach.

When it was over, my family cheered, and I ran to the phone. I called Wil.

"That was awesome!" I said.

"I know," she said. "I know. I've got Penny and Molly on the other line."

I said goodbye and told her I'd see her tomorrow. I hung up the phone with a smile on my face. Everyone in my family felt as happy as me. The phone rang again and I picked it up, hoping it was one of the Ballplayers or Sleepy.

"Hello?" I asked.

"Hi," a man's voice said. "This is Frank from the realtor's office. Is Mr. Jones there?"

I handed the phone to my dad and returned to my spot on the couch. I crossed my arms in front of me as my mother tried to make small talk with Natalie and my father took the phone into the other room. After a few minutes I retreated to my room where I could return to my normal miserable self without getting into trouble. As I sat tossing the ball in and out of my mitt, I couldn't handle the stress anymore. I had to talk to someone. I needed a friend to listen and tell me we weren't going to move, and that my life wasn't going to be over.

I sneaked out of my room and tiptoed into the master bedroom. I picked up the phone. As I dialed my best friend's number, I started to question why he hadn't called me after seeing the report on our football league on television.

"Hi, Sleep," I said.

"Hi," he replied.

"Did you see the news?"

"Yeah," he said.

I paused, waiting for him to give us a compliment. He said nothing.

"What did you think?"

"It was cool," he mumbled.

I opened my mouth to force out some more small talk, but my best friend cut me off. "I gotta go," he said. "I'll see you at school tomorrow."

I hung up the phone with a bad feeling. My brother stepped into the room.

"I'm going out," he said. "I'll see you later."

I buried my head in my mother's pillow.

"What's wrong, kid?" Rico asked.

"Everything," I moaned.

"Talk to me," he said.

"Sleepy's acting weird. I don't think he likes me anymore. He's my best friend. What am I gonna do?"

"He's not mad at you," Rico said.

I looked up at him curiously. "How do you know?"

"He's going through some tough times," my brother explained.

"Like what?" I asked.

"Maybe you should ask him," Rico said.

"I have," I replied.

Then I stopped and thought of all our brief conversations. They were about moving, football, and how much I hated to do homework.

"Be a friend, kid," my brother explained. "Sleepy needs one—now more than ever."

Chapter Sixteen

I set my alarm a half hour earlier than usual. When it went off at seven A.M., I didn't even think of hitting the Snooze button. I got up, put on my clothes, stuffed my book bag, ate breakfast, and headed out the door. Just before I slipped out of our house, my mother scurried into the living room.

"Where are you going?" she asked.

I could tell by her wide eyes that she thought I was running away.

"I'm going to see Sleepy," I said.

"Why?" she asked.

I shrugged. "Rico says he needs somebody to talk to."

"About what?" she asked.

I shook my head at my mother. "You're being nosy," I muttered as I walked out the door.

I ran straight to my best friend's doorstep. The door creaked open.

"What are you doing here?" Sleepy asked.

"I woke up early."

I stepped quietly inside. I sat down in the living room and waited for my best friend to finish packing his bags. He rubbed his sleepy eyes and grunted as he piled his books in his bag.

"Is everything all right?" I asked.

"Yeah," he mumbled.

I waited for a second and chose my words carefully.

"I'm your best friend," I said softly.

He looked at me and rolled his eyes.

"All right," I admitted. "Maybe I haven't been acting like one lately. But I want to know what's eating at you."

Before Sleepy could answer, a tall man appeared in the living room. My eyes looked straight up at him. His muscles bulged inside his tight T-shirt.

"Keep it down," the man said. "Your mother is sleeping."

I quickly turned to Sleepy, begging him to identify this very large man taking up a large portion of the room. Sleepy simply muttered, "Sorry." He picked up his bag and said, "We're leaving anyway."

I peeked up from under my cap as Sleepy trudged down the stairs.

"Who was that?" I asked.

"My father," Sleepy replied.

My nerves tingled all over my body. A lump formed in my throat. Sleepy had never known his father. He never talked about him. I didn't even know if his father was still alive.

"I'm sorry, Sleep," I muttered.

"For what?" he replied.

I didn't know what to say.

"My father's back," he said. "I'm supposed to be happy. I'm supposed to be thrilled."

We walked together and I listened.

"He's being all nice to my mom and sister," he said. "But how do we know how long it's going to last before he leaves again?"

"How does he treat you?" I asked.

"He's all right, I guess," he replied.

Neither of us had any answers. We both agreed that adults could really drive kids crazy. I thought about all the times I complained to Sleepy about my dad and about moving. My problems felt so small compared to Sleepy's.

"Sorry for being such a lousy friend," I said.

"It's not your fault."

"I just thought you were getting sick of me," I told him. "With Pete the Creep and all the other guys always teasing you about my playing sports and being your friend."

"I don't care what they say," he assured me.

"You sure?" I asked.

He nodded. "'Cause I know if I wimp out on you, you'll hunt me down and tackle me."

I grinned, "You've got that right."

Later that night my father came home. I forced a smile and said hello. I had started to accept that I would have to make a minor attitude adjustment in order to survive the move. If Sleepy was strong enough to get through his situation at home, I would have to find a way to get along with my father, too.

"I have something you'll be happy about," my father said.

My heart skipped a beat.

"What?" I asked.

He rested his briefcase on the ground and loosened his tie. "I'd like to tell you and your mother at the same time."

"Maaa!" I screamed as I moved to the end of my seat.

My mother emerged from the bathroom.

"What?" she asked.

"Dad has something to tell us," I said. "He says it will make me happy."

"This I've got to hear," my mother said. She sat down on the couch next to me.

"Go ahead, Dad."

He slowly pulled off his shoes and socks. Then he pushed back in his reclining chair. "The deal fell through."

I couldn't have dreamed it any better.

"Really?" my mother gasped.

"Yeah," my father said in disappointment. "The company decided that it didn't need two people for the position. They gave the job to someone else."

He closed his eyes and took a deep breath. I sank down in my seat, torn between feeling bad for my dad and relieved that I had reclaimed my life. My mother walked over to my father, bent over, and gave him a kiss on the cheek. "I'm sorry," she said softly. "I know how much you wanted it."

A few minutes of silence passed. My father started snoring in his chair, and I stood up. I walked up to him and watched his chest rise and fall. I held my breath and twisted my hands in my shirt. Then I whispered, "I'm sorry." I tiptoed into the kitchen to talk to my mother.

"Well," she said. "You got what you wanted."

"I know," I said.

"Then how come you're not doing cartwheels?" she asked.

I shrugged. I looked over at my father and saw how tired he was. All the weeks of work and stress were hitting him at once. I went into my room and flopped down on my bed. I thanked God that I wasn't moving. Then I felt the shame of saying "I." I apologized and thanked God that our family wasn't moving. I told him that I believed everything would still work out.

Then I went into my parents' room and picked up the phone. I called the Ballplayers one by one.

"Must have been the crickets," Molly joked.

"Your wish came true," Angel said.

"I knew it would all work out," Penny assured me.

Then I called Wil and told her to return all the going-away gifts.

"We already did," she said. "It was all part of Operation I'm Not Moving. I never doubted the plan."

"Yeah, well, I did," I said.

"Don't sweat it, Ro," she said. "You're a Ballplayer for life no matter where you end up."

"Well, I'm glad I'm still here," I told her.

"So am I because we have a national title to win on

146

Sunday," Wil said. "And we can't do it without a shorty like you."

I laughed.

"Tell Rico I'm dropping off the scouting report tomorrow," she added. "We need to have a meeting."

I assured the commissioner that I would relay the top-secret information to our head coach as soon as I saw him. After I hung up the phone, I finally called the one person whom I needed to talk to the most.

"Hi, Sleepy," I said when my best friend answered.

"What's up?" he asked.

"We're not moving."

"Really?"

"Yeah."

"How come you're not excited?" he asked.

"I don't know," I said. "I guess I'm just relieved. I wish Rico were around so I could tell him myself."

"Yeah," Sleepy said. "He'll be glad you're staying."

"How's your dad?" I asked.

"All right," he said.

"Are you hanging in there?"

"Yeah," he said. "The best I can."

I wanted to give him a motivational and inspirational pep talk, but I wasn't like Wil. My words and thoughts were simple and never flowed easily. I never seemed to say the right things at the right time.

"Thanks for being my friend," I mumbled. "I'll see you tomorrow."

As I hung up the phone, my insides filled with energy and hope. I would see my best friend and the Ballplayers for many more days to come. I never thought feeling so low and scared would make me feel so thankful. I took out a pad of paper and left Rico a note.

Dear Rico,

I know I've been a pain over the last few weeks and I just wanted to say I'm sorry. I really hoped that I could be the first one to tell you that we aren't moving, but you weren't here. I wanted to jump up and down and celebrate with you, but now I feel kind of dumb for getting so worried about everything.

I miss you when you're not around, and I was scared if we moved I wouldn't see you or my friends again. I'll try and be a better sister and a better friend. I'll even try and be a normal daughter before Mom and Dad kick me out. Wake me up when you come home. If you don't get this note until tomorrow, don't forget about our football game on Sunday. Wil needs to talk to you about the scouting report.

Your favorite sister,
Rosie

Chapter Seventeen

I walked the halls of Lincoln School all day as if I were as big as Mr. Gordon. No longer did I count down all the laughs, arguments, and good times. Lincoln was my school again.

"You'd better have your homework done," Miss Lopez warned me as I strolled into her room. I proudly pulled my assignment and held it up in front of her with a satisfied grin.

"My, you're in a good mood today," she said.

"We're not moving."

She came up and gave me a hug. I stood there as stiff as a board, but adrenaline rushed through me. With my favorite teacher off my back and my family staying put, I could breathe easy again.

When the last bell rang, I ran out into the hallway. Mr.

The Broadway Ballplayers

Gordon's voice slowed me down, but my heart kept thumping. I couldn't wait to catch up with Sleepy so we could go down to the park and throw the football around. I had to be ready to play for our first national title on Sunday.

"I bet twenty bucks that they're gonna lose," I heard Pete the Creep call out. I pushed through the crowd and stopped right next to the Ballplayers. Pete stood staring at Sleepy as he unloaded his books. "What, are you scared?"

"Are you deaf?" Wil shouted. "I told you, gambling is not allowed in the League. Give it up, Pete."

"You don't even have twenty bucks," Molly quipped.

Penny walked up to all of us with a big smile. "What's going on?"

"Pete wants to bet on our game," Wil explained.

"You're betting on us winning, right?" Penny asked.

Pete didn't answer. He shrugged as Penny kept talking to some passers-by, asking if they were coming to the big game on Sunday. I watched Pete as he humbly walked away.

"Hey, Pete," Penny called out in a friendly tone. She ran over to him and reached out an open palm. "See you on Sunday."

He stared at her hand and then looked away. Penny extended her palm farther and said, "Come on, man. It's a big game."

He reached out and slapped her five. Then he turned and walked away.

With all the commotion in the hallway, I was one of the few who saw what Penny did that day. Instead of despising Pete, a chill shot up my spine in admiration of Penny. She had earned the right to keep her title as the coolest kid on Broadway Ave.

"If you want to see some heart and guts," Wil called out to anyone and everyone who had ears, "come to the park Sunday at two."

We spent the next twenty-eight hours making signs, writing letters to family members, and calling city officials and the media.

"I feel like one of us is running for president," Molly joked.

"I will be someday," Wil added surely. "But for now all we need to win is some respect."

Tasha's Trashers looked about twenty pounds heavier than they had the previous weekend. Wil checked all their names and numbers to make sure they hadn't flown in any stars from out of town for the title game.

"We don't need to cheat to win," Tasha scoffed.

On the sidelines I turned to Sheila, our friend, who had put up with Tasha for four weeks. She had missed last weekend's game because she'd had the flu.

"You feeling better, Sheila?" I asked.

"Yep," she said with a warm smile. "Good enough to kick your butt."

I grinned back at her and she winked. "You're going down, Ro!" she said as I jogged onto the field with the Ballplayers. We huddled up at midfield and screamed so loud my ears kept ringing for a few seconds.

"What are we made of?" Wil called out.

"Heart and guts!" we all screamed.

Rico and the coaches huddled on the sidelines and called out the starters. The referee blew the whistle, and we took the field for the kickoff. The crowd roared. Although Wil gave us specific instructions not to pay attention to all the hype, my curious eyes couldn't help but wander up and down the sidelines. I spotted all the kids from our hallway, Mr. Gordon, Miss Lopez, Rico's friends, my mom and dad, and of course, my best friend, Sleepy. When he saw me look over to him, he flashed a big smile.

Penny and I lined up to receive the kickoff. Tasha called out, "It's coming to you, Shorty!" just as the ball descended in the air.

"It's pancake time!" another Trasher added.

The ball thumped into my hands, and I squeezed it so hard I thought it was going to pop. I gritted my teeth and bolted forward. I followed my wall of teammates, but slowly the wall started to crumble. I traveled about twenty yards and then ran into Sheila and Tasha. I bobbed and weaved but felt like I was trying to climb out of a black hole. Tasha jumped on my shoulders and down I went.

"Nice run, kid!" my brother called out.

"Go left next time!" my father yelled.

"Heart, Rosa! Heart!" added my mother.

Penny led a strong offensive attack down the field. We were within ten yards of scoring when Molly caught a sweet pass and then had the ball stripped. The ball popped out, and the Trashers pounced on it.

Our fans moaned in disappointment. We tried to strike back, but the Trashers caught us all on our heels.

Catch Shorty by Rosie

They marched down the field and right into the end zone.

"Come on!" Wil screamed. "We can't play this game again!"

"Let's take it to 'em!" Molly added.

In the third quarter we finally put some points on the board when Penny ran a quarterback sneak right into the end zone. But that was the best we could do. I caught a few passes and dodged one or two tacklers on each play during the fourth, but we couldn't drive the ball down the field far enough. The Trashers were everywhere.

"Who's got the heart and guts now?" Tasha said in the last few seconds of the game. The final whistle blew, and we trudged off the field dripping with sweat, tears, and charcoal. I took off my helmet and sucked in the cold fall air. Wil went down on one knee and held her head in her hands. I walked over and patted her on the back.

"I wanted to win this game for you, Ro," she said.

While none of us were content with the loss, not one tear came to my eye. Miss Lopez walked up to me and rested her hand around my shoulder.

She smiled as people in the crowd gave both teams a standing ovation. Most of the kids from Lincoln School rose to their feet. Then a skinny little head popped up in the middle of the crowd. Pete the Creep didn't clap or cheer. He simply picked himself up off his seat and stood without heckling any one of us.

Sleepy jogged over and gave me five. Then he crinkled up his nose and said, "Man, you stink."

The Broadway Ballplayers

I pulled off my equipment and handed it to my mother. She bent over and kissed my sweaty hair. My dad started to comment on the game. He went over all the things we did and did not do. I looked up at him and just nodded.

For once, win or lose, I had no complaints. I was still a Ballplayer at home on Broadway Ave.

About the Author

by Meghan Holohan

I was the typical little sister, and Maureen was the typical big sister. I went through her room, read her diary, and listened in on her telephone conversations. She called me a pain and hardly ever let me hang out with her friends. We were sisters being sisters, but somewhere along the way I grew up and realized that Maureen is not only my best friend in life, but also the person I admire most.

Many people name superstar athletes or famous movie stars as their favorite role models. But I always believed that a role model should be someone you see and interact with on a regular basis. It may be one of your parents or another close relative. It also could be a great teacher or coach. Whomever you choose, make sure it is someone who goes after a dream and refuses to let anyone or anything stand in his or her way.

When I think about the way Maureen lives her life, I reflect back on her senior year of high school. During a basketball tournament over Christmas break, Maureen suffered a serious knee injury. Doctors believed her season and possibly her career were over. After two months of rest and rehabilitation, Maureen played in her team's sectional playoffs. She rejoined the starting lineup, hoping to lead her team to a second consecutive state championship. Minutes into the second game of the tournament, her injured knee buckled again. She completely tore a ligament and would need surgery in order to play basketball again.

I remember sitting in my family room about two days after Maureen had knee surgery. It was a cool, windy afternoon in March. I could hear a familiar noise out in our driveway. It was the sound of a basketball bouncing. I opened our garage door and went outside only to find my sister sitting on a stool with a bulky knee brace on and crutches lying next to her. She shot baskets while neighborhood kids chased down her rebounds. Right then I knew no one was ever going to hold my sister back from any of her dreams.

Maureen has taken that same amount of passion and determination she had while playing basketball and has transferred it over to her latest dream, which is *The Broadway Ballplayers.* I've seen her start her business in a tiny sunroom, work for hours behind a computer, and speak in front of hundreds of children and adults. She's called me from hotel rooms in some of the 100-plus cities she's traveled to in about a year and a half. Her mission is to give you something we never had as kids—stories about strong girls who have a passion for sports and life.

It still amazes me that most people in the book business rejected this idea when Maureen started two years ago.

If only they had seen her in our driveway . . .

Meghan Holohan played basketball and earned a master's degree at Rider University.